# Yuletide Hero

## JANE BLYTHE

# Acknowledgments

I'd like to thank everyone who played a part in bringing this story to life. Particularly my mom who is always there to share her thoughts and opinions with me. My wonderful cover designer Amy who did an amazing job with this stunning cover. My fabulous editor Lisa for all the hard work she puts into polishing my work. My awesome team, Sophie, Robyn, and Clayr, without your help I'd never be able to run my street team. And my fantastic street team members who help share my books with every share, comment, and like!

And of course a big thank you to all of you, my readers! Without you I wouldn't be living my dreams of sharing the stories in my head with the world!

# CHAPTER

*One*

December 19th
10:52 A.M.

This was the worst part of her job.

Hayley Hood loved being a social worker. She loved being able to make a difference in the lives of children who were unfortunate enough to not get the start in life they deserved. She couldn't imagine doing anything else with her life.

Except on days like today.

On days like today when she was going to remove a five-year-old girl from the only home she had ever known, her job really sucked.

*You're doing the right thing.*

There were some days when she needed that reminder.

Just because she knew she was doing the right thing—the only thing she could do under these circumstances—it didn't make it any easier.

Kinsley Turner would be traumatized. She wouldn't understand, she would cry, and beg for her mommy and daddy even if they had been hurting her. But Kinsley had to be removed from her home, after what they suspected her father had done, she couldn't remain there. They had to take her somewhere she would be safe.

Hayley would make it as easy as possible for the child, and maybe one day Kinsley would accept that it had been for the best.

But that day wouldn't be today.

Today, she would mourn the loss of her family.

She pulled her car to the curb outside a small, dilapidated two-story house. The yard was a mess as was the car parked in the drive. The house was rented to Jay and Maria Turner. Jay had been in and out of prison on a myriad of domestic violence and alcohol-related charges and was currently unemployed and living on welfare. Maria hadn't held a job for longer than a couple of weeks, mostly due to constantly having to take time off to heal from the injuries inflicted on her by her husband.

A police cruiser pulled in behind her car, and a little reluctantly, Hayley climbed out of her own car. Taking a child from their home was bad enough, but doing it just a few days before Christmas was so much worse. Right now, Kinsley should be getting excited about the impending visit from Santa Claus. She should be thinking of flying reindeer, twinkling Christmas trees, and opening presents on Christmas morning.

Instead, she would be spending the holidays in a foster home.

If she was lucky a good one, if she wasn't then possibly a place worse than the one they were about to remove her from.

"You ready to do this, Hayley?" Detective Adam Abram asked as he and his partner climbed out of the car. Adam was a couple of years older than her, with brown hair and brown eyes. He was a good cop and a nice guy, and they had worked together a few times before. Adam's partner was Jessica Spears, a year older than her, she had frizzy red hair and large green eyes, and while Hayley didn't have a lot of friends, she definitely counted Jessica amongst them.

"I guess so," she answered Adam's question.

"You know this is for the best," Jessica said, shrugging into her coat as she rounded the car.

"I know. Kinsley can't stay here, she's in danger, but that doesn't make this any easier to do."

Both detectives gave her sympathetic looks. They knew her past, *everyone* knew about her past and why she had decided to become a social worker. She knew better than most people did what it was like to be a child in a bad home. She had been one of the lucky ones, she'd been adopted and grown up in a wonderful home with amazing parents and a fabulous extended family.

Hayley prayed that Kinsley would be as lucky.

"Let's just get this over with," she muttered as she shrugged into her coat and followed the cops up the concrete path to the front of the Turner's house.

This wasn't the first time she had removed a child from their home, and she knew it wouldn't be the last, but she hadn't gotten used to doing it. She probably never would. There had been some children she'd had to drag away kicking and screaming and crying for their parents, the cuts and bruises from being beaten by those very same parents still fresh on their little bodies.

Jessica rapped on the door, and the three of them waited in silence.

The wait amped up her agitation, and by the time the door was finally opened, her hands were shaking so much she had to clutch them together so nobody noticed.

"Mr. Turner, I'm Detective Abram, and this is my partner Detective Spears. This is Hayley Hood, she's a social worker, we're here to take Kinsley," Adam announced.

Jay Turner just stared at them but even from a couple of feet away Hayley could feel his anger.

Not just anger.

Fury.

They already knew what this man was capable of. He wasn't to be underestimated. Adam and Jessica knew that, and she noticed that both of them had their hands hovering over their weapons.

"You can't take my kid," Jay snarled at them. He was drunk, she could see it in his face, hear it in his voice, and smell it on his breath.

"We can, sir," Jessica informed him, holding out the paperwork. "Based on your daughter's statement, the bruises that were seen on her body, and the suspicious nature of your older daughter's death, we are removing Kinsley from your custody at least until the conclusion of this investigation."

"You can't take my kid," Jay repeated, making no move to take the paperwork she offered.

"Please step back, sir," Adam said. "Don't make this worse for Kinsley than it's already going to be."

"We will handcuff you, Mr. Turner, if you don't step back, and if necessary, we will arrest you," Jessica warned.

With another glower, Jay Turner finally snatched the papers from her hand and took a step back allowing the three of them to enter the house. Inside, the house wasn't any cleaner or tidier than the outside had been. Ripped carpet, peeling wallpaper, piles of garbage littered about, dirty laundry scattered on the floor and the table, filthy dishes piled high in the kitchen sink.

There was a small, tattered Christmas tree in the corner, and Maria Turner stood beside it, Kinsley in her arms.

Jessica nodded at her. "You get Kinsley," the cop directed.

Shooting Jay Turner a wary look, she walked further into the house and over to the mother and daughter. "Hey, sweetie." She gave the little girl what she hoped was a reassuring smile. "My name is Hayley. You're going to come with me for a little while, okay?"

"How come?" the child asked. Although too thin for her age, Kinsley was a pretty little girl. She had long brown hair that had been pulled into two messy braids and large, long-lashed, blue eyes, and a light smattering of freckles dotted her nose and cheeks.

"Well, my friends, Detective Abram and Detective Spears have to sort things out with your daddy and your mommy, and it's better if you're not here while they do that."

"Oh," Kinsley said.

"Hey, I have a great big, cuddly teddy bear in the car waiting for you," she told the little girl. She always brought along something for the children she removed from their homes. It wasn't something she had to do for her job, just something she wanted to do for these kids.

"Can I keep him?" Kinsley asked, all excited.

"Sure can, that's why I brought him. Come here." She reached out to take the child, and Maria Turner took a step back. Leaning in close she whispered in the woman's ear, "Don't make her see you handcuffed with a gun pointed at you." Reluctantly, the girl's mother released her grip on her daughter, and Hayley took the child, balancing her on her hip and heading for the door.

"Right behind you," Adam told her as she stepped outside.

Hayley nodded and hurried for the car. Kinsley wasn't wearing a coat, and she wanted to get the child out of the cold as quickly as she could. "So, what are you going to name your teddy bear?"

"What color is he?" Kinsley asked.

"He's brown."

"Is he a boy or a girl?"

"Whatever you want?"

"I think it's a ..." Kinsley trailed off, obviously deciding. "A boy."

"Okay," Hayley said as she put the little girl into the car seat and began to buckle her in.

"I think his name should be Brownie because Leah and I used to make brownies sometimes," she said as she picked up the bear and held him in her lap.

"That's a great name." She smiled at the child, who was holding up extremely well considering she had just been taken from her parents. "I'm just going to close your door and get into the driver's seat, then I'm going to take you to the house you'll stay in for the next few days, okay? Once we get there we can play for a bit, and there'll be lots of other kids for you to play with too."

"Will I have my own bed?" Kinsley asked.

"Yep, you sure will."

"Leah and I used to share a bed."

"At this house you and Brownie will be able to share a bed, just the two of you."

Kinsley nodded, and Hayley straightened and closed the door. She was just walking around the car when she heard footsteps pounding toward her. Just as she turned to see what it was, a large body slammed into her, knocking her backward, then landing on top of her as they both went sprawling onto the pavement.

It was Jay Turner, screaming obscenities as he swung a fist at her, connecting with the side of her head hard enough that she saw stars.

He raised his fist again, but before he could deliver a second blow, he was knocked sideways by Adam. Jessica knelt at her side, helping her up.

Maria Turner stood in the doorway of her house, crying. Kinsley Turner sat in the backseat of her car, crying, and as the cold wind blew and her cheeks stung Hayley realized that she was crying too.

She had certainly been right when she thought this visit would end in tears.

~

1:04 P.M.

Brian Xander paced nervously up and down Hayley's front porch.

When he'd heard what had happened at the Turner house, he dropped everything and came straight here. Hayley was a great kid, and he hated that she had been hurt.

No.

Not a kid.

She was no longer the quiet, shy little girl who cried a lot. The little girl who was like an old woman in a small child's body was gone. In her place was a beautiful young woman who was smart, compassionate, and adored her job.

A job that could have gotten her killed.

That terrified him.

The two of them had been friends for so long. He'd been eleven and Hayley five when she was adopted by close family friends, so they had pretty much grown up together. Their families had gone on vacation together several times, and they'd spent holidays together—Christmas, Easter, Fourth of July. She had always been a part of his life, and he didn't want anything to ever change that.

Good friends could be hard to find and once you had found one you wanted to hold onto them and never let them go.

"Where is she?" he muttered aloud.

With a grandfather who was a cop, and two uncles who had also joined the police force, Brian couldn't deny that he had been tempted to follow in their footsteps. His father was a doctor, and there had also been the temptation to follow him into the medical field.

Instead, he had found a compromise between cop and doctor. He had completed medical school and come to work with his Uncle Ryan and Hayley's mother Paige Hood who were three-way partners, along with Brady Crowley, in a private security firm. They had thought that having a doctor as part of their team would be good for when they had to deal with clients who had been injured, but because they were in danger and in need of a bodyguard, it wasn't safe for them to go to a hospital.

Since he often worked in dangerous situations, he was a trained bodyguard. He knew how to shoot a gun and hit his target, he was trained in self-defense and martial arts. He worked on a case-to-case basis so because he sometimes had stretches of free time, he also volunteered his services at a free clinic and at the center for abused women and children that his aunt and some family friends ran together. It made for a busy life and a lot of patients with a range of different physical and psychological conditions.

Right now, there was one patient in particular he wanted to see.

Hayley.

Brian yanked his phone from his pocket and punched in Hayley's name. He was just about to press call when her car pulled into the driveway.

He had crossed the yard in five steps and was pulling open her door before she had even turned off the engine. "Are you okay?" he demanded, perhaps a little more forcefully than he should have but his heart hadn't stopped hammering in his chest since he'd heard what had happened.

"What are you doing here?" she asked.

"I asked first," he snapped.

Hayley laughed. "Okay then, well if we're still nine and we're still doing that then, yes, I'm okay. Now, your turn."

"I'm here to see you," he replied like it was obvious. Why else would he have stopped what he was doing and come right over?

"Why?" Hayley reached over and grabbed her bag from the passenger seat, then gently nudged him out of the way so she could get out of the car.

"Why?" he spluttered. "Because I can see a lump on the side of your head from here."

"Didn't my mom tell you I went to the hospital?"

He trailed her back to the front porch, so close on her heels he was practically attached to her.

"I didn't think I needed to go," Hayley continued, unlocking the door. "But Adam and Jessica insisted. They called another social worker to take Kinsley Turner to a group home, then they took Jay Turner down to the station and booked him while I went to the hospital. You know that I don't have a concussion or anything." She turned to look at him. "I wanted to go back to work and check on Kinsley, but my boss made me take the rest of the day off."

That should have reassured him.

But it didn't.

The only thing that was going to reassure him was checking Hayley out himself.

"Go and sit down," he ordered.

"What?" Her large blue eyes widened even further at his sharp tone.

Great. He was scaring her. Last thing he wanted to do after the day she'd had. Brian forced himself to calm down. "Please," he said deliberately gentling his voice. "I just want to examine you."

"The doctor at the hospital already did," she reminded him.

That wasn't enough for him right now. "Please."

Obviously reading his desperation, she shot him a reassuring smile. "Okay, if it will make you feel better."

"It will." He took her elbow, closed and locked the door behind them, and guided her into the living room and down onto the couch. He sat beside her and picked up her wrist to take her pulse. Which was normal. Pulling a stethoscope from his bag he pressed it to Hayley's chest. Her breathing and heart rate were also normal.

Taking her chin between his thumb and forefinger he tilted her face to the side so that he could examine the lump on her head. Looking at it gave him a lump in his throat. Hayley was lucky that she hadn't been knocked out when that lunatic had attacked her for simply doing her job. He probed the bump as gently as he could. When Hayley winced, he let his fingertips trail down the side of her cheek.

"You were lucky," he murmured.

"I was," she agreed, her voice soft and a little distant.

"Were you hurt anywhere else?" Brian asked, his gaze still locked on the lump on the side of Hayley's head.

"A couple of bruises from hitting the ground when he knocked me down. Really, it's nothing. I'm fine."

"Fine," he echoed.

Slowly his eyes moved from the bump up to meet Hayley's eyes that were watching his every move.

For some reason his gaze dropped to her lips.

Kiss.

The word flew into his mind.

That was the last thing he'd been expecting.

You didn't kiss the friend you'd had since you were eleven.

It was wrong.

Wrong.

Definitely wrong.

And yet it didn't stop him from wanting to do it.

"Brian? Is something wrong?"

The words startled him, and he jerked away from her, dropping his hands to his sides.

Hurt flashed momentarily through Hayley's eyes, but she masked it well. "Are you okay?"

"Fine," he said briskly, shoving the stethoscope back into his bag. "I was just thinking how glad I was that Adam and Jessica were there and Adam was able to get Jay Turner off you as quickly as he did before he could inflict any more damage."

"That's why they were there, in case anything goes wrong. It was the first time I've ever needed the help," Hayley said, her own tone brisk. "Are you convinced that I'm all right now?"

"Yes." He offered her a small smile. "Sorry, I just got a scare when I heard what happened. It's not that I don't trust the doctors at the hospital, it's just that when it's your friend you kind of want to be sure."

"Don't worry I won't tell your dad you didn't trust him to do his job," she smiled, but it seemed strained.

"Dad? Why was my dad the trauma surgeon treating you in the ER?"

"Because it's Mark and he likes to be in control, kind of like you do," she teased.

"I guess I can be kind of a control freak sometimes," he agreed a little sheepishly. Bossiness kind of ran in his family. While his Uncle Jack was well known as the bossy one of the three Xander brothers, they had definitely all been painted with the same brush. As the oldest, not just of his siblings, but the oldest of all the cousins as well, he had received the biggest dose. "Sorry about that."

"It's okay, it's kind of sweet, and I guess friends just worry about friends." She shot him another strained smile then stood. "Not to push you out the door or anything, but I have a headache, and your dad said I should try to get some rest so I'm going to go lie down for a while."

"If you have a concussion you shouldn't go to sleep here alone."

"Then it's lucky I don't have a concussion. Really, Brian, there is no need to worry." She unlocked the door and held it open.

Gathering his bag, he stood and walked out the door, pausing on the porch. "I'm going to call in an hour to check on you."

"It's really not necessary."

"Necessary or not, I'm going to call in an hour to check on you. Sweet dreams, Hayley."

He could feel her eyes on him as he walked down the garden path and to his car parked on the street outside her house. It wasn't until he had driven off down the road that he realized his heart was still hammering in his chest.

Only now it was for a whole other reason.

Wrong thing to do or not, he still wanted to kiss Hayley Hood.

4:19 P.M.

"Are you okay?" Sophie Xander asked without preamble as she rapped on the door, and her best friend Hayley opened it.

"I wish people would stop asking me that." Hayley sighed.

"I think when you're attacked at work and get taken to the hospital in an ambulance it's a reasonable question," she said wryly. She and Hayley had been friends since they were five years old, making it twenty years next year. In some ways it felt like just yesterday that they were two little girls and she had made it her mission in life to help Hayley adjust to a normal life and a normal family after the horrible start in life she'd had. In other ways, it felt like they had already lived a lifetime in those twenty years.

"I suppose," Hayley conceded.

"Who else has been asking you that? I mean, besides the doctors."

"Are you going to stand out there on the porch in the cold all afternoon?" Hayley asked, ushering her inside.

Sophie smirked. "I bet I can guess who."

"Oh yeah?" Hayley asked all innocent as she went and sat on the couch where she had obviously been curled up with a book until Sophie had arrived.

"Don't play that innocent act with me." Sophie went and joined her on the couch. Picking up a cookie from the plate, she nibbled on the corner of the gingerbread man's arm. "From the way your cheeks went all bright pink the second I mentioned who else had been asking how you were it is a dead giveaway that Brian was here earlier."

"He dropped by for a moment," Hayley acknowledged, refusing to meet her eye.

"I knew it." Sophie clapped her hands delightedly. Her best friend had had a crush on Sophie's oldest cousin for the last decade at least. Brian was her Uncle Mark's oldest son and was six years older than her and Hayley. Her friend thought that Brian saw her as nothing but a kid, a friend and nothing more. Sophie wasn't so sure though. She saw a spark between them. All Brian needed to do was take off his friends glasses and see Hayley for the beautiful, smart *woman* she was. Not a kid any longer.

"It's nothing to be so excited about."

"Are you kidding?" Sophie exclaimed. "Brian drops whatever he was doing to rush straight over here to make sure you were okay, that is totally romantic."

"It might have been," Hayley said slowly, "if he hadn't made a point of saying that he was only here to check on a friend."

"You don't believe that, do you?" That was crazy, both of them were crazy. Hayley should just tell Brian how she feels, and Brian should just open his eyes and see that Hayley wasn't a kid anymore and that they would be perfect for one another.

"It's what he said."

"It might be what he said but how did he say it?"

Hayley's blue eyes went far away, and her friend didn't need to say anything to answer that question.

"He said it like there was something more to it, didn't he?" Sophie asked.

"Not exactly."

"But," she prompted when Hayley didn't continue. Her tone said there was more she wanted to say but hadn't. They were best friends, they told each other everything, always, no holding back, no secrets. Over the years, they had shared everything from their fears and anxieties to their crushes and their highest highs and lowest lows.

"He said he came because he wanted to check me out. He took my pulse, then listened to my chest, then he looked at the lump on my head, and I don't know, his face, it looked like he felt something. And then our eyes, they kind of locked, and I was sure he was thinking about kissing me. But he didn't. He just said that he was glad Adam and Jessica had been there and that he was here to check on me because that was what friends did."

"You thought he wanted to kiss you though?" So many times she had wanted to just tell her cousin that Hayley liked him, but she had promised her friend she wouldn't, and they always kept their promises to each other.

"I *thought* so," Hayley hedged. "But it's not like I'm an expert in men."

"And I am?" Sophie huffed a mirthless chuckle.

"At least you've been in love before."

"Yeah, and that worked out so well." She had been in love—or at least thought she had been—twice before, and both times the boys had turned out to be killers. After the second time, she had sworn off relationships. That was nearly ten years ago, and she hadn't dated since.

Nor did she ever see herself dating.

Her heart just couldn't take another beating like that again.

Being single might be lonely, but at least it was safe.

After some of the things she'd been through, safe was nothing to be sneezed at.

"I'm sorry, Soph." Hayley reached out for her hand. "That wasn't nice of me to bring that up."

"It's okay."

"No. It's not. I know you're still not over it, but I hope that one day you will be. I don't want to see you end up alone because of two guys who didn't deserve you. They didn't even deserve to live."

And one of them hadn't.

One of them was dead now, the other in prison, but the scars they had left behind were still fresh and raw, and Sophie wasn't sure they would ever fade enough for her to be able to move forward with her life.

"I love you, Soph, you know that. You know I'm always here for you," Hayley said.

"I know you are, but I want you to be happy. Just because I can't move on doesn't mean you shouldn't. You should tell Brian how you feel."

"I can't." Hayley dropped her gaze to her lap.

"You can," she contradicted.

Hayley just shook her head.

They were still holding hands, and Sophie lifted them up so Hayley could see the small stump on each of their hands where their pinkie fingers had been before they'd been chopped off by a psychopath out for revenge against their parents. "If you're strong enough to survive this then you're strong enough to do anything. Even take a giant leap of faith and find out if you and Brian could work out."

"That was different," Hayley protested. "That was survival. When we were in that basement, we did what we had to do. Just like before I was adopted, my sisters and I did what we had to to survive. This isn't the same."

"Yes, it is. This is survival too, just a different kind of surviving. You deserve all the happiness in the world, Hayley. You were abducted as an infant, grew up in a house with a monster who abused his other victims, and would have done the same to you when you were older. You want what your parents have, and if Brian is the one then you should do something about it. Do you want to let fear hold you back and watch him fall in love with someone else? Do you want to miss out on your chance? Your family and mine are friends. Can you spend the rest of your life watching him with someone else knowing that maybe you two could have been together?"

"No," Hayley said softly.

"Then do something about it."

"I'll think about it if you do the same. If I can overcome the messed-up stuff that's happened to me then you can too. You were right there with me in that basement, and you survived. You've survived every horrible thing life has thrown at you, which means you're strong enough to find a way to put it behind you and find happiness. We'll do it together. Deal?"

Hayley was wrong.

She wasn't strong.

What life had thrown at her had cut too deep.

Sophie didn't know how to move on.

She wasn't even sure it was possible.

But if Hayley needed to hear her say that she would so she could give herself permission to be happy then she'd agree to the deal.

"Deal," Sophie said, lying to her best friend for the very first time. "So, tell me about the case that started this mess." She pulled her hand from Hayley's and gestured at the large lump on the side of her friend's face.

"Thirteen-year-old Leah Turner was found dead under suspicious circumstances. Then her five-year-old sister drew a picture at school that made her teachers concerned. They spoke with her and found bruises on her back. We were called in, and I was the one assigned to the case. There was definitely cause to remove the child from the home, and with the father's violent history we were worried that it wouldn't go smoothly. And it didn't."

"Understatement of the century," Sophie said with a small laugh.

She'd had enough of talking about the deep stuff for one day. Hayley stood a chance at having happiness if she would just tell Brian that she liked him, that was all that mattered. "How's the little girl doing?"

As she listened to Hayley talk about Kinsley Turner, she felt herself relax.

Safe really wasn't so bad.

Really.

It wasn't.

~

7:32 P.M.

Something woke her.

Hayley blinked and groggily opened her eyes.

It was dark, and she couldn't remember where she was.

She wasn't lying in her bed, and from the shadows surrounding her it looked like she had fallen asleep on one of the couches in the living room. After Sophie had left, she'd intended to just rest her tired eyes for a couple of minutes then go and cook something to eat, take a long, hot shower, and go to bed. Exhaustion from the day's events must have gotten the best of her, and she'd fallen asleep.

Yawning, she reached over to the coffee table and fumbled about for her cell phone. When her fingers brushed against it, she picked it up and glanced at the time. Seven thirty, she'd been asleep for almost two hours. It was really too early to go to bed, but she was tired, and she had a headache, so may as well head upstairs.

There was a missed call on her phone.

Brian.

He'd called once already—just like he'd told her he would—while Sophie was still here which had started up round two of her friend's lecture about telling Brian how she felt about him. She must have slept right through the second call. It was a wonder he hadn't driven back over here and battered down her door to check up on her.

It had been almost fifteen minutes since his call. If she called him back now, she'd probably preempt another visit. It wasn't that she didn't want to see Brian it was just that she was too tired right now to deal with that.

Hayley was just about to dial when she heard a thump, then the sound of shattering glass.

Startled, she staggered to her feet.

What was going on?

Was it one of her windows that had just broken?

A bird flying into it?

No, it was winter, already well past dark, and the birds had already settled for the night.

Something else had broken her window.

Cell phone still in hand, Hayley was running toward the back of the house where it sounded like the window had broken when her front window shattered.

Whatever had been thrown through the window was on fire.

Flames danced about and quickly latched onto her carpet.

She looked down in the direction the other window had broken and saw the orange glow of fire.

Someone was throwing rocks wrapped in material soaked in something flammable and set alight into her house.

Twice.

This wasn't an accident.

Another rock shattered her other front window, and Hayley ran upstairs. Flames were consuming the downstairs of her house far too quickly, and someone was out there who was trying to kill her, so even if she got out the door, she wasn't safe. At least upstairs she could hide out until help arrived.

Help.

She had her phone and quickly dialed 911 reporting the fire and that the cops were needed as well.

"Hayley."

Someone called her name, but it wasn't a voice she recognized. Hayley moved to her bedroom window, and when she looked out her heart dropped.

Jay Turner stood in her front yard.

It didn't take a genius to figure out why he was here and what he wanted.

He was here to kill her.

She had taken his daughter away, and now he was going to take her life away. The cops and fire department would be on their way, but it would be a few minutes at least before they arrived.

She might not make it out of this house alive.

Brian.

Her mind immediately flew to Brian and a need to tell him goodbye filled her. As much as she loved her parents, her little sister, her best friend, and the rest of her family, there was only one person she couldn't die without talking to one last time.

"Not such a tough girl now, are you," Jay Turner mocked. Even from up here, she could see the smirk on his face and the malevolent glint in his eyes.

Determined not to give him what he wanted, Hayley stepped away from the window so he couldn't see her anymore. Quickly she dialed Brian's number.

"You missed my call," he said as soon as he answered.

"Brian," she whimpered, it was all she could get out. Smoke was slowly starting to infiltrate the upstairs, and as much as she tried to keep it together, she could feel herself starting to unravel.

"What's wrong?" he demanded, reading the fear in her voice.

Tears pricked her eyes, but she fought them back. Just a couple of hours ago she and Sophie had been talking about her past. She had survived more in her twenty-four years than most people would in an entire lifetime, and she wanted to believe she could survive this too, but she wasn't sure.

"Hayley? What's going on?"

"Jay Turner is here," she murmured. It was silly, she knew he couldn't hear her, he was outside in her front yard, but still she felt the need to be quiet.

"What do you mean? Where? At your house?"

"In my yard."

"Call the cops," he said, sounding more panicked than she felt.

"I did. He's—" she broke off as her bedroom window shattered when another rock came through it.

"What was that?" Brian asked, having obviously heard the breaking glass.

"He's throwing rocks wrapped in material that he set on fire into my house," she said, backing away from the burning rock that had landed on her bed and set it on fire.

"There's nowhere to hide, Hayley," Jay shouted from outside.

"Get out of there. Now," Brian ordered in her ear.

"There's nowhere to go," she said. "The downstairs is already alight. I came upstairs to wait for the fire department, but now it's burning too. Even if I get outside, he's out there."

Brian muttered what sounded like a curse. "The garage," he said.

"What about it?"

"If you go out the spare bedroom window you can get onto the garage roof. Is Jay Turner in your front yard or back yard?"

"Front."

"Jump off the garage down into the back yard. If you can distract him somehow, make him think you're still in the house then he won't even notice. He should run as soon as he hears sirens. He's already in a lot of trouble, he's not going to want to get caught setting fire to your house."

"How do I distract him?" she asked. Her mom was the cop, not her, she didn't know what to do in a situation like this.

"Do you still have the mannequin?"

"Yes."

"Put it in the window in the bathroom, he'll think you're in there, then get out the spare bedroom window as quickly as you can."

"Okay," she agreed. There was so much she wanted to say, but she felt overwhelmed. She'd had a crush on Brian Xander since she was nine years old. So many times she had wanted to tell him how she felt but had been afraid because she knew he thought of her as just a kid, then as they'd gotten older just a friend.

Just as she was about to say something she heard the sound of another window being broken.

It had to be the other bedroom window.

The one in the room she wanted to escape through.

She didn't have any time left.

"Goodbye, Brian," she said, and hung up before he could say anything else. Then she shoved her phone into her pocket, grabbed the mannequin from the hallway closet and carried it into the bedroom.

The smoke was getting thicker, and she was sure it was affecting her breathing, but adrenalin was flooding through her system, and she was too busy trying to survive to worry about it.

With the distraction in place, she ran to the spare bedroom, the rock had landed on the floor near the window it had come through, and the flames hadn't spread far yet so she could easily make it to the other window.

Ripping a pillowcase off one of the pillows on the bed she wrapped it around her fist then slammed it through the glass.

Without pausing, she scrambled through, and just as she dropped down onto the garage roof, she heard another window breaking. Jay must have fallen for the mannequin in the window trick and thought she was in there.

Taking advantage of his distraction, she crawled to the edge of the roof and jumped down. Landing awkwardly, Hayley rolled a few times before coming to rest under her favorite tree. It was tall, the tallest in the area, and in the fall it was a blaze of autumnal glory. In the summer it was so leafy and a perfect place to sit in the shade and read a book and drink a glass of homemade lemonade. Right now, its bare branches reached way up into the dark winter night sky, snow was falling thick and fast and had already piled up on the branches.

Hayley pushed herself up into a sitting position and rested wearily against the sturdy trunk.

Then she heard it.

The best sound in the world.

Sirens.

~

8:00 P.M.

. . .

"Where is she?" Brian demanded as he parked his car down the block and ran through the maze of police cars and fire trucks that filled Hayley's street.

"We have people going in to look for her," the closest firefighter said, indicating the people heading toward the door.

Brian shook his head. "She should be out."

"How do you know that?" the man asked sharply, looking at him suspiciously now.

"I was on the phone with her. I told her to go out the window and onto the garage roof because the man who did this," he waved a hand at the burning house, "was still outside. She set up a diversion so she could get out." At least he hoped it had worked, but she'd hung up on him.

After telling him goodbye.

The kind of goodbye you said to someone when you thought it was going to be the last time you ever spoke with them.

Was it goodbye?

Would that be the last time he ever talked to Hayley, or had she gotten out of the house in time? If she'd gotten out had Jay Turner caught her and killed her or dragged her off with him to torture her before he killed her?

"I'll tell my men," the firefighter said and headed off to do that.

Alone, Brian didn't hesitate, just ran around to the side of the house, jumped the fence, and scanned the backyard.

Over by the tree, a figure sat propped against the trunk.

There was no doubt in his mind that it was Hayley.

Relief had him wanting to grab her, hold her, and give thanks that she was alive and had managed to make it out of the house. But her house was still on fire, and she was sitting too close to it, so he ran over, snatched her up, then ran with her back around to the front of the house and into the street.

Someone saw him coming and opened the back door of the nearest patrol car and Brian slid Hayley inside, climbing in beside her and closing the door.

Then he just stared at her.

Her eyes were open, and he didn't see any blood.

Until he looked closer.

"Hayley, your hand." He gently reached out and lifted it. It was streaked in blood, the majority of which seemed to be coming from a long gash running down her ring finger, over her knuckle, and along the back of her hand.

"I must have cut it when I broke the window to get out," she said. "I didn't even notice."

"Adrenalin," he mumbled, more to himself than to her. If she hadn't noticed the cuts on her hand, what other injuries hadn't she noticed? "Where else are you hurt?" he asked briskly. He wanted to draw her into his arms and hold her, but his emotions were bubbling too close to the surface, it was so much easier to fall into doctor mode.

"Umm," she said slowly, her blue eyes were round, and while clear she was clearly struggling to comprehend what had just happened. At least she was falling apart now and not while she'd still been trapped inside her burning house.

"That's okay." He forced his voice to come out calm and not betray the terror over what could have happened that was swirling inside him. "Let me look." His eyes met hers, seeking her permission and when she nodded, he began to run his hands over her body, searching for injuries.

There were a few cuts on her palms and knees from where she must have scrambled over the broken glass in the window getting out of the house. She seemed to be tender on her hip and shoulder, and one of her ankles was a little swollen, probably from landing awkwardly when she jumped off the garage roof.

All in all, she was extremely lucky.

Again.

His eyes moved to the stump on her right hand where her pinkie finger used to be and then to the lump on the side of her head from earlier today.

Hayley had survived the first five years of her life in a house of horrors, then an abduction as a teenager by a psychopath who had killed half a dozen other people. Would she survive Jay Turner?

Would he?

Brian lifted his gaze to find her watching him with a funny expression on her face. He knew what she was thinking. He knew that she had a crush on him, that she had for years now. Back then she'd just been a kid, he was six years older than her, and it wouldn't have been appropriate for the two of them to date.

But now ...

Now, Hayley wasn't a kid anymore. Now she was a gorgeous, smart, caring, courageous woman.

Why hadn't she ever told him how she felt?

Was she waiting for him to make the first move?

"Hayley," he started.

"Hayley," someone else said at the same time, flinging open the car door and dragging Hayley out.

"I'm okay, Mom," Hayley said, but he heard the wobble in her voice as she was folded up in her mother's arms.

"Xavier called as soon as he was alerted to a problem at your address," Paige Hood told her daughter, clutching her tightly. He had known Paige and her husband Elias most of his life. She had dated his Uncle Jack for a little while before marrying her husband and had been his Uncle Ryan's partner for close to two decades when they were both cops. Now she and Ryan ran a private security firm together. Paige had been injured by a violent stalker and left unable to have children and had adopted Hayley and Arianna when he was eleven. Ever since, Hayley had been a firm fixture in his life.

"You said on the 911 call that it was Jay Turner, are you positive?" Ryan asked, standing behind Paige and Hayley, surveying the still-smoldering house.

"Yes. I saw him, and he talked to me," Hayley answered. "Now my house and everything in it is gone."

"No, sweetheart," Paige told her daughter. "Dad spoke with one of the firefighters, and they said whatever accelerant he used wasn't very strong, the fireballs left some damage to the floors and carpet, and your bed is ruined, but that's it. Water damage is also minimal. Does she need to go to the hospital?" Paige looked to him.

"No," Brian replied. "She might need some stitches and a few bandages, but that's it."

"Let's go then. Brady and Sawyer are waiting for us at the office, and I told Adam and Jessica to meet us there if they need to question you,"

Paige said, ushering her daughter away from the hubbub and into another car.

Brian followed, he wasn't letting Hayley out of his sight. That man was still out there, still a threat to Hayley, and he didn't see him backing off until he got what he wanted.

Hayley dead.

The ride to the offices was quiet. Ryan drove, Paige held her daughter like she never wanted to let her go, and he sat and stared at Hayley like if he didn't watch her she might disappear.

"I'll grab the first aid kit," he announced as they joined the third partner in the security firm, Brady Crowley, and another bodyguard Sawyer Watson, who were waiting for them in the conference room. He had a feeling he knew where this little meeting was heading, and he knew how he wanted things to turn out.

"We weren't able to find Jay Turner," Ryan was saying when Brian returned to the conference room. "He must have run when he heard the sirens, but he didn't go back home."

"So, he could come after me again," Hayley said.

"No." Paige shook her head emphatically.

"No," Brian echoed, picking up Hayley's hand and beginning to clean away the blood so he could see the extent of the damage and attend to it.

"Am I going to go and stay with you and Dad?" Hayley asked her mother.

"I wanted you to, but then Ryan pointed out that if Jay Turner could track you down and find out where you live, then he could easily find you at our place," Paige explained.

"So where am I staying?" Hayley looked a little suspicious now.

"Somewhere he won't think to look for you," Brady replied.

"With me," Sawyer added.

Hayley shook her head.

Brian shook his head.

"No," they said simultaneously.

"You and Ashley have children. What if he found me there?" Hayley elaborated.

"You can stay with me," Brian said. "I can be your bodyguard."

She gave him that funny look again. "I'll probably be fine on my own. I don't think he'd be stupid enough to try anything else."

"You *will* have a bodyguard," Paige said like it was already decided.

"I appreciate you wanting to do it, Sawyer," Brian told his friend. "But Hayley's right, you and Ashley have two little kids, and it's Christmas, you don't want to leave them now to stay at one of our safehouses. Hayley will be safe with me, I'm trained as a bodyguard, and a doctor, so I can keep a check on her wounds as they heal. There's no reason that Jay Turner should think to look for Hayley at my house."

"Hayley?" Paige looked to her daughter. "That sounds like the perfect solution. What do you think? Are you happy to have Brian as your bodyguard and stay with him until the cops get Jay Turner in custody?"

Hayley looked conflicted, and for a moment he thought she was going to say no.

But then she nodded slowly, her eyes meeting his and searching them as though trying to seek the answers to the questions that were in her head. Whatever she was looking for she must have found because she finally said the words he wanted to hear. "Okay. Brian can be my bodyguard."

~

10:48 P.M.

"Do you want to go straight up to bed?"

"Hmm?" Hayley blinked and looked up to find Brian staring down at her. She had no idea what he'd just said even though she'd heard the words, her brain had kind of checked out, overwhelmed by everything that had happened.

"You look exhausted. Do you want to go right up to bed?" Brian repeated.

As tired as she was, she was also wired. She didn't think she was going to be able to fall asleep. "Actually, I'm a little hungry."

"Dinner it is." Brian took her elbow and guided her into the kitchen, pulling out a chair at his table for her. "What do you want?"

She shrugged. "I don't care. Anything is fine."

"What about some mac and cheese?"

"Sounds good."

Brian got busy cooking while she sat at the table and stared aimlessly around the room. She'd been to Brian's house plenty of times before, the downstairs was one big open plan living space, the kitchen in one corner, a large dining table that actually sat most of their families was next to it, then there were three couches grouped around a widescreen TV, and a pool table and foosball table beside them.

Over the years, they'd had a lot of fun times hanging out here together with their family and friends, laughing, playing games, eating, and just enjoying being together. Those times had been both wonderful and sad. She always had so much fun with Brian, but each time they hung out, it just served to remind her that he thought of her as a kid, a friend, another little cousin.

She wanted to be so much more.

But you didn't always get what you wanted.

Hayley knew that.

If you did, she would never have been abducted as an infant and kept prisoner for five years. She never would have been abducted as a teenager and had her finger cut off, and someone wouldn't have tried to kill her tonight.

Hayley didn't want to be here in Brian's house. She didn't want him to be her bodyguard. She had almost said no when they'd been discussing it back at her mom's offices. But the only other option would be having someone else as her babysitter until Jay Turner was caught. Which meant having to stay with Sawyer and his wife Ashley—endangering their young children—or stay in one of the safe houses and take Sawyer away from his family at Christmas.

Neither was a viable option as far as she was concerned.

This meant for the foreseeable future, she was stuck here with Brian.

Stuck wasn't quite the right word.

Under other circumstances the two of them spending all this time alone together would have been a dream come true, but at the moment, there seemed to be this tension between them. She didn't know why. As far as she was concerned nothing had changed, but obviously Brian felt differently because he kept giving her the strangest of looks.

"Eve dropped off some clothes for you. Tomorrow your mom is going to go through your house and pack some more things for you, but these should do for tonight. Why don't you go take a shower, change, choose which bedroom you want, and by then the mac and cheese should be ready."

"Yeah, okay," Hayley agreed. It was better than just sitting here wondering why Brian was acting strange and worrying that Jay Turner would track her down. "That was nice of your sister."

"She was happy to do it. You know she loves a chance to go through your wardrobe even if she can't fit into any of your clothes at the moment."

Brian's younger sister Eve was three years younger than him and three years older than herself, and was currently seven and a half months pregnant with her first child and huge. Eve's twin sister Elise had recently given birth to her first child, a little girl, and Hayley knew that Eve was hoping to have a girl as well, but so far, the baby had been uncooperative every time she'd had a sonogram, and they hadn't been able to find out the gender.

It must be so exciting to have a new life growing inside you, something that was half of you and half of the person you loved. She wanted to have a big family one day, lots of kids, lots of love, and lots of fun. Hayley knew that a part of her mother still wished she had been able to have a biological child, just like she knew that her mom loved her fully and completely even though they weren't biologically related. In the nearly twenty years she had been Paige and Elias Hood's daughter, she had never once doubted that she was loved.

Hayley hoped one day she'd turn out to be even half the mother that her mom had been.

But not today.

Right now, she wasn't ready for kids.

"I'll text her later and tell her thank you," Hayley said as she stood up and took the bag of clothes Brian held out. "Is there any bedroom you prefer me to take?"

"The one at the end of the hall, furthest away from the stairs, next to mine, that way if Jay Turner does somehow manage to track you down here and comes after you again, if he breaks in, I'll be between him and you."

"Okay," she said. It was odd seeing Brian like this. All bodyguard like. She knew that he was a trained bodyguard and that he worked for her mom at the private security firm, but she'd never seen him in action before. He was so brisk, his face all harsh and stern, his gaze constantly roaming the room even though it was only the two of them here and Jay Turner had no way of knowing this was where she was staying.

Although she didn't turn around, Hayley could feel his eyes tracking her as she walked across the room and up the stairs. She let out a breath of relief when she reached the second floor, being scrutinized so carefully made her feel self-conscious.

Heading for the room that Brian had told her to take, she set the bag of clothes down on the bed and closed the curtains. A hot shower, dinner, and then bed sounded pretty good right about now. Was she allowed to take a shower with the stitches on her hand? Brian had told her to take one but she better check.

"Brian?" she called from the top of the stairs.

"Yeah?"

"Do I have to be careful of the stitches in the shower?"

"No. I put a waterproof bandage over them. I'll change it before you go to bed and make sure the wounds are dry and clean."

"Okay." That was the Brian she was used to, doctor Brian.

Turning the water as hot as it went, once the bathroom was full of steam she stepped under the spray. The water worked wonders on her sore muscles, washing away all the stiffness and soreness from being knocked down and then jumping off the roof.

By the time she stepped out of the shower and wrapped a fluffy white towel around herself, Hayley was feeling a lot better. It shouldn't take too long for the cops to find Jay Turner and then she could go back to her normal life. Hopefully, it wouldn't take long to repair the damage to her house, and if she was lucky, she might even be able to be home before Christmas.

"You look better," Brian said as she came back downstairs.

"I feel better," she agreed.

"Good." He offered her a smile. It was a little strained but a smile nonetheless. "Dinner is ready."

"It smells amazing." She drew in a deep breath through her nose.

"Hope it tastes as good as it smells." Brian set two bowls down at the table and took a seat.

"It will, you know you're an amazing cook."

"Thank you," Brian said, he didn't meet her gaze, and his tone felt a little forced.

"Mmm." She sighed as she took her first bite. "This is so good. Thank you for cooking me dinner."

"Of course."

They both lapsed into silence as they ate. For the first time, Hayley felt uncomfortable around Brian. Back when she was a teenager, sometimes she'd find herself blushing and unable to talk whenever it was just her and Brian, but she hadn't done that in years. Now she felt like that awkward teenager all over again.

What had changed?

Was it just that Brian was worried about her and taking his job as her bodyguard seriously enough that he couldn't think about anything else?

No. That couldn't be it because he had been looking at her funny before that. Back in her house when he'd come to see her right after Jay had attacked her at the Turner house, she'd thought he wanted to kiss her.

Was that what had changed?

Had he figured out that she was secretly in love with him, and he was obsessing over how to let her down gently?

Despite her feelings for Brian, she didn't want anything to ruin their friendship. She loved hanging out with him, and she didn't want to lose that just because he didn't see anything more between them than friendship.

"Let me check your hand."

Brian was kneeling in front of her, and she stared at him trying to figure out what was going on behind those cool blue eyes of his. When he picked up her injured hand his touch was so gentle as he checked her hand and changed the bandage.

When he was done, he didn't let her go.

His fingers curled around hers, and he stared at their joined hands as though he wanted to say something, but he didn't.

After a full minute he stood and slowly released her hand. He leaned in and for a second Hayley was sure he was going to kiss her, but then he touched his lips to her forehead.

"Goodnight, Hayley. You should go up to bed now, you need some rest after everything you've been through today. I'll be down here, and then in the room right next to yours. Jay Turner won't get to you again. Sweet dreams."

Abruptly, he turned and started to clean up in the kitchen, leaving Hayley staring after him more confused than ever.

# CHAPTER
*Two*

December 20th
2:43 A.M.

No one took what was his.

No one.

His daughters were his property. What he did with them was no one else's business. Taking Kinsley was unacceptable, and he *would* make sure that the child protective services lady paid for that.

Jay Turner thumped the steering wheel of his car in frustration.

He didn't think she had died in the fire. When he'd heard the sirens, he'd had no choice but to run. He hadn't gone far though. His car was parked further down the street, and he'd watched for a little while before it had become too risky, and he'd had no choice but to drive off. But before he had he thought he's seen Hayley Hood.

When the idea to set fire to her house had occurred to him, he'd thought that the flames would take hold much quicker than they had and that the house would be a raging inferno by the time fire trucks arrived. But it hadn't worked out that way. The rocks wrapped in cloth that he'd set a match to seemed to have fizzled out shortly after he'd thrown them through the windows. He should have used an accelerant, but he'd been in a hurry, eager to exact his revenge. Such a simple mistake but one that had saved the woman's life.

If it was the last thing he ever did that girl would be punished.

Not just killed but punished before he ended her life.

Punished in the most horrific way he could think of. Burned alive hadn't worked out, but Jay was sure he could think up something equally as horrible as befitting messing with what was his.

His kids, his wife, they belonged to him. His home was his castle and there he was king. His wife was there to attend to his needs, prepare his meals, do his laundry, and keep the children out of his hair. The children were to be seen and not heard, and when they needed a reminder of that he was all too happy to give it to them. What business was it of anyone else's if that reminder included physical punishment? As a kid he had been beaten whenever he broke the rules, it hadn't done him any harm, it was the way of the world.

Tracking Hayley Hood down hadn't been hard. He knew her name from when she came to his house and took his kid. All he had to do was a couple of simple searches and he found her. If he had been able to find her once, he'd be able to find her again.

That wasn't what was worrying him.

Thanks to that obnoxious woman, his kid had been taken, and now he couldn't even go back home. Where was he supposed to stay? It was winter, snowing outside, it wasn't like he could stay in his car, he'd freeze to death. But if he went back home he'd no doubt be arrested, his bail revoked, and he'd be spending Christmas in the local jail.

He hit the steering wheel again.

He wanted to wrap his hands around Hayley Hood's neck and squeeze the life out of her. He wanted to hit her over and over again until she understood that nobody told him what to do and nobody controlled him.

Jay had half a mind to track her down right now and finish what he'd started.

Hayley Hood wasn't the only one who would be getting punished.

That kid of his would be getting a beating when she came back home. If the stupid thing had just kept her mouth shut about what had happened to her older sister, then none of this would have happened. Leah had had a smart mouth on her, she'd thought that she could talk back, she thought that she could defy him, she had thought that she was worth something.

He had taught her.

He would teach all of them.

His wife was no better. Maria was supposed to be in charge of the children, and yet she seemed incapable of controlling them. Leah hadn't learned what a woman's place was, and neither had Kinsley. Child rearing was the mother's responsibility and if Maria couldn't even do that then what good was she? When he got his hands on her he was going to teach her a lesson she would never forget.

Those interfering cops and CPS people might be monitoring his wife's cell phone, but when he found somewhere to hide out, he was going to risk calling her. It might be a while before he could get his hands on Kinsley or Hayley Hood, but he needed to do something to release some of the anger building inside him, and Maria was going to take the brunt of it. It was her place after all.

Jay was getting tired of driving around and around. He had to find somewhere to spend the night. He needed some sleep if he was going to find out where the social worker was hiding.

There.

He slowed the car and pulled it over to the side of the road.

Perfect.

That was just what he had been looking for.

Parking his car, he got out and strode up to the house before him. It was a building site, but it looked like it was mostly finished. He should be warm enough inside. He could crash, get a couple of hours sleep, and be gone before the workers returned later this morning.

Inside it was cold, but not unbearably so. If he was lucky there might even be hot running water. Heading straight upstairs he found the bathroom and tried the taps. Water. Hot water.

Shedding his clothes, he left them where they lay and stepped into the shower. The hot water felt amazing, and he started to relax. Hot water. That was an idea. He wondered what it would be like to burn someone inch by inch with boiling water. Jay sneered, maybe he'd try that out on Hayley Hood.

He wasn't really a killer, but he was willing to make an exception where that woman was concerned. He was willing to rip her to shreds. He had never been this angry with another human being before in his life.

He'd thought that Leah possessed the ability to get under his skin and drive him insane until all he could think about was slapping that smirk off her face and silencing that mouth of hers, but this social worker was something else. Hadn't she ever been taught to keep her nose out of someone else's business?

When he was done with her, she was going to realize just what a mistake she had made.

Only by then it would be too late.

If he didn't kill her, what kind of example was he setting for Kinsley?

She would grow up thinking that she could do as she wanted. That she could be defiant and didn't have to listen to him and give him the complete obedience that he demanded.

That was unacceptable.

He would not have his daughter thinking such things.

He would kill Hayley Hood for what she had done, then he would get his kid back and teach her and her mother a lesson that would wipe away the bad example the social worker had set.

So many possibilities.

So many ways to hurt that witch.

He would make her wish she had burned to death in her house.

When he was finished with her, she would pray for Hell, and still he wouldn't send her there.

The water that streamed down him began to run cold, he had lost track of time daydreaming about all the ways he could torture Hayley Hood before he killed her.

Shutting off the water, since there was no towel to dry himself with, he left his clothes on the floor and walked to the window, staring out at the night sky. It might be two in the morning, but Christmas displays still tinkled and shone in front yards. Jay had never really liked Christmas. He'd never understood the getting something for nothing mentality or this goodwill toward men nonsense that people were always spewing.

But this year he liked the idea of a gift under his tree.

That gift being Hayley Hood's dead body.

"I'm coming for you, Hayley," he said into the night. "I hope you know that. I hope the idea terrifies you. I hope you don't get a second's peace. I hope you can't sleep because you know I'm going to find you in your dreams, and then I'm going to track you down, kill anyone who tries to stop me, and make you suffer. I'm going to relish every second of it, your screams, your tears, your blood, they're mine, just like your life is mine. There's nowhere to hide. Wherever you're holed up I will find you. I can't wait to see you soon."

∾

5:11 A.M.

Nothing relaxed Hayley more than sewing.

The machine's whirring as she pushed the material through was soothing. She could let her mind wander and let go of all of her fears and insecurities and just be.

She remembered the first time she had ever done any sewing. She was six years old, and she'd been with her parents for almost a year. It was Halloween, and her mom had been hand-making all of their costumes. It was the first holiday she'd celebrated as a Hood that she had been really excited about, the others had all incited various degrees of anxiety.

But not Halloween. She'd liked the idea of dressing up and pretending to be someone else. She'd liked the idea of being able to see monsters and know that she didn't have to be afraid because maybe then she would stop being afraid of the monster that had kidnapped her and pretended to be her father for the first five years of her life.

It had worked.

After that, she hadn't been as afraid anymore.

Part of that was because of the bonding she and her mom had done in the days before Halloween. She'd wanted to help make her little sister's costume, and she and her mom had sat together in the same chair, her mom at the back, her perched in front, and sewn Arianna's costume.

Ever since that day sewing had been her happy place.

As a little girl she'd been a dancer, and as she got older, she had also started sewing dance costumes for herself and her fellow dancers. Even now, though she hadn't danced in years, she made the costumes for her old studio.

When she wasn't sewing dance costumes, she made Christmas gifts for the people she loved. In the past, she'd made stockings, teddy bears, patchwork quilts, tablecloths, napkin holders, door wreaths, angels, and door stoppers. This year she was making little Christmas cloth books, they were adorable, and although they'd taken her pretty much the whole year to make, she was so proud of them.

Between making dance costumes and handmade gifts for family and friends most of the time when she wasn't at work, doing housework, or running errands, she was sewing. But right now, when she was stressed and scared and needed to do it she couldn't because all of her stuff was back at her house. She didn't even know what condition it was in. She knew her mannequin was probably destroyed, but all of the gifts she'd already made for Christmas could be as well. The sewing machine she'd received as a gift from her parents for her sixteenth birthday might be ruined. She knew it was only a thing, that it could be replaced, but it was special to her, and she didn't want it to be gone.

"It's five o'clock in the morning. Why are you up?"

Hayley turned from the window where she had been staring out at the falling snow and daydreaming. Brian was standing behind her, dressed in nothing but a pair of gray sweatpants that hung low on his hips.

He looked good.

*Really* good.

Had he always been this toned or had he been working out more recently?

She hadn't dated a lot because she wasn't very confident when it came to intimacy, and she wasn't very experienced, but right now all she wanted was to be upstairs, in bed, naked, with Brian's hands touching her everywhere.

Hayley felt her cheeks heat.

Was her mouth hanging open?

Was she staring?

She was making a fool of herself.

"You okay?" Brian watched her with a small smirk, and she knew that he knew what she was thinking.

Was he going to remind her that they were friends and let her down gently?

When she was being honest with herself, Hayley knew she didn't just have a crush on Brian Xander. She was in love with him. Maybe she did need to hear him admit point blank that all they were ever going to be was friends so she could finally let go of her feelings and move on.

She cleared her throat and then said, "I'm fine."

"Couldn't sleep?" He came to stand beside her.

"No. I got an hour or two, but then I couldn't get back to sleep. I got tired of tossing and turning so I thought I may as well just get up."

"Did you have nightmares?"

"No. I don't think I dreamed at all." Thankfully, she didn't suffer from nightmares and never really had. She knew her mom had been worried that she would have had bad dreams when she first went to live with them, but other than the occasional one, mostly after she had been kidnapped when she was fifteen and again later that same year when she had been in an explosion, she'd never really had them. Her mom suffered from them regularly, even decades later, and knowing what they did to someone she was really grateful she hadn't been afflicted.

"How are you feeling?"

"Fine. A little sore, but it's nothing major. I don't even need to take any Tylenol or anything. It's more just a dull nuisance than anything else."

"Don't be a martyr though, if you start hurting later then take something."

"I will," she agreed. "You can go back to bed if you want."

"If you're up, I'm up," he said.

Right.

Because he was her babysitter for the foreseeable future.

Hayley would love to say that she didn't think Jay Turner would be stupid enough to make another attempt on her life and that they were all blowing this way out of proportion, but unfortunately, she couldn't do that. She had taken away his daughter, and while that didn't bother the man in the normal paternal sense of having his child taken away from him, especially on the heels of his other daughter's death, it angered him because he thought of Kinsley as a possession. *His* possession, and she had messed with that. He wouldn't stop until he killed her.

"Sorry," she told Brian. She didn't want to be a bother or a burden to anyone.

"Don't be sorry. None of this is your fault. You were just doing your job. The cops suspected that Jay Turner had killed his older daughter and was abusing his younger one. That little girl wasn't safe there, especially after what we now know about him. I'm happy to be here for you when you need it." He reached out and took her hand.

The second he touched her she felt that same jolt flash through her she always felt whenever he touched her.

This was a mistake.

Being here.

She was only letting her feelings grow and giving herself false hope. She should have agreed to let Sawyer Watson be her bodyguard. Christmas was still a week away, surely that would have been enough time for Adam and Jessica to find and bring Jay Turner into custody. Then Sawyer could have been back home for Christmas with his wife and kids, and she wouldn't be here, in Brian's house, drooling over his half-naked body and wanting the two of them to make out.

"So, what do you want to do today?" Brian asked.

Make out.

The words were on the tip of her tongue and very nearly slipped out before she could stop herself.

"I can't do what I want to do. I want to do some sewing, and finish the last of the Christmas gifts, but my sewing machine and the pattern and all the material is back at my house. If it even survived the fire."

"You're in luck," Brian said. He still held her hand and began to drag her toward the door to the garage, his blue eyes twinkling merrily.

"Why?"

"Because Brady and Sawyer dropped off something last night after you went to bed. They got your sewing machine, the boxes you had in your sewing room, and another little surprise."

"A surprise?" Surely that was enough. Her dad was a firefighter, and she wasn't surprised he had wanted to make sure that she had her sewing machine, he knew that it was what she did to relax and that she would certainly need it right now. But that and the material would have been enough. What else had they brought?

"One you're going to love." Brian grinned at her as he opened the garage door and gently pushed her inside.

Hayley couldn't do anything but smile too when she saw what Brady and Sawyer had brought over for her.

∾

8:51 A.M.

"We need to find where Jay Turner is hiding out," Adam Abram said, frustrated as he sat down at his desk.

As the father of a four-year-old little girl, he hated the idea of a man who beat his kids being out there somewhere. His wife had died when Claire was just a baby, so he had been a single parent most of his daughter's life. He knew what it was like to be tired, stressed, and trying to fit the role of two parents into the few hours a day he got with Claire. His job often had him working unpredictable hours, if he didn't have a supportive family, he didn't know how he would cope. At the end of a long day, he was often exhausted, and his bundle of energy little girl didn't have an off button. There had been many times when he'd almost lost his temper or been tempted to just send her to bed instead of playing with her and enjoying the time they had together.

But he didn't.

Because his daughter was the very center of his world and all that he had left of his wife. He loved her more than she could ever know, and there wasn't anything she could do that would make him strike her.

"Thinking of Claire?" his partner asked.

"Yeah." He knew that Jessica understood exactly how he was feeling about this wife beating, daughter killing man they were hunting because she was a single mother as well. Her husband had bailed on her and their son Freddie a couple of months before the little boy's second birthday. Freddie was five now, and Claire's best friend, he and Jessica took turns looking after the kids one weekend a month to give each other and their respective families a break.

"We have to find evidence that he killed Leah," Jessica said.

Adam shook his head. "Before we do that, we have to find him. Leah is dead, and Kinsley is safe in a foster home, but as long as Jay is out there Hayley is in danger."

"There is an APB out on his car, and a BOLO out on him. We can't just drive around and around the city hoping that we happen to see him. We've done everything we can to make sure that he'll be found. Right now our focus has to be the case, proving that he killed his daughter."

As much as he hated to admit it, Jessica was right.

For the moment, Hayley was safe with Brian, every cop in the city was searching for him—not just because of what the man had done but because Hayley's mother had been a cop, and the lieutenant was a family friend of the Hoods and no one messed with part of the cop family and got away with it—there was nowhere Jay could hide. Their job was to find the evidence they needed to keep Jay Turner in prison when he was found. Hayley's statement that he had tried to kill her should be enough, but he wanted the man to pay for killing his daughter as well.

"All right, let's go over what we have so far," he said to his partner.

"It was the coroner's report that first led us to believe that Leah Turner's death wasn't the accident her parents claimed it was," Jessica said, rifling through the stack of papers on her desk and pulling out the report. "Jay and Maria claimed that Leah was trying to sneak out of her room in the middle of the night because they wouldn't allow her to see her boyfriend, and she slipped and fell off the roof."

"The medical examiner found injuries that were inconsistent with a fall. Numerous old broken bones dating back to when she was a toddler suggested abuse, especially given her father's violent past with his wife. And there were the recent injuries, a broken nose and cheekbone. According to the ME they were less than twenty-four hours old."

"And the marks on her shoulders and wrists," Jessica added.

"We suspected that her father had chased her up onto the roof, caught up with her, held her around the wrists, and dangled her over the edge of the building before finally shoving her by the shoulders off the roof." Just thinking about it was enough to get his blood boiling. What kind of fully grown man attacked a thirteen-year-old girl? Everyone they had spoken to had said that Leah was quiet and shy, but very sweet and a polite kid, she hadn't deserved what her father had done to her. Even if the teenager was a nasty, rude, mean-spirited kid, she wouldn't have deserved what her father had done to her.

"Then we talked to Leah's friends at school. None of them knew anything about a boyfriend. They said that Leah wasn't confident around the boys in her class, and although a lot of them were interested in her and thought she was pretty, she didn't date. She focused on her schoolwork because she wanted to be able to get a scholarship to college so she could get away from her home."

"From all accounts, Leah wasn't a troublemaker, and it seemed unlikely that she would be sneaking out of her bedroom window in the middle of the night."

"Unless her father had broken her face that evening after school and she'd had enough and decided to run away," his partner suggested.

"Doesn't seem to fit with the profile," Adam countered. "If she was going to leave, I think she would have just gone to an adult and told them what was going on. And she was smart. I think she knew her father would probably receive minimal prison time, be ordered to enter some sort of rehab, and then even if she'd been put in foster care, she would be sent right back home for the abuse to start over again. She wanted out permanently, that's why she was already thinking about college. Besides, I don't think she would have left her little sister behind and alone at the mercy of their abusive, alcoholic father."

"Which brings us to Kinsley."

"Right." He nodded, thinking of the little girl and the look on her face as her father had darted past him and Jessica and run down the path to the street, slamming into Hayley. The child had been understandably upset, and it had taken him and Jessica a while to calm her down. Kinsley was only a year older than Claire and had already been through so much in her short life.

"The day after Leah's death, she drew a picture of her house with her sister lying dead on the ground and her father on the roof. Her kindergarten teacher knew about Leah's death, and when she saw the picture, she thought it was odd Kinsley had put her father on the roof and asked her about it. Kinsley said that her daddy had been on the roof arguing with Leah and then Leah fell. The teacher noticed bruises on Kinsley's wrist, and when she asked the little girl, she said her daddy had done it. She immediately called CPS and the precinct to tell us what Kinsley had told her."

It had been three days since Leah Turner fell—or was pushed—to her death and two days since Kinsley had told what she knew. A day since they had removed the child from her home afraid that she was in imminent danger of being harmed, and Jay Turner was still a free man. At first, they had nothing but a crayon drawing and a story from a five-year-old told secondhand through her teacher, not enough to get an arrest warrant. Yesterday they'd had the man in custody, but he'd gotten bail claiming he was just a desperate father driven into a blind rage at having his only remaining child ripped away from him.

But Adam knew that was a lie.

Jay Turner didn't care about his children in the way most fathers did. To him, they were merely possessions that he could do whatever he wanted with. They—specifically Hayley—had taken Kinsley away from him, he couldn't do anything but try to finish what he started and kill Hayley.

They needed to find him before he tracked her down and took a second shot at her.

Right now, they only had one definite way of getting the proof they needed that Jay had killed Leah.

Kinsley.

The injuries and marks on Leah's body were circumstantial. Any defense lawyer could invent a story about how she came to have them, possibly blaming the imaginary boyfriend. The only way to prove murder in court was Kinsley's account of what she had seen and heard that night.

"We need to speak with the social worker assigned to Kinsley Turner, make sure she has a lawyer appointed to her, and then we need to make a time to go and interview her." Adam wanted Jay Turner in prison before Christmas Day so at least Kinsley could begin the process of moving on. Who knows, maybe with husband and father out of the way Maria and Kinsley's lives would be better. Then he wanted to go home and enjoy Christmas with his own little girl.

12:33 P.M.

"You ready for lunch?"

"Not yet." Hayley looked up from what she was doing. "We're not finished yet."

"Silly me," Brian said with a smirk. "Of course, we can't stop to eat until we're finished assembling your Christmas village, even though we've been working on it for six hours now and haven't stopped for a break."

Hayley couldn't help but laugh. "Hey, usually this takes me a whole day or more to get everything just right. Six hours and we're nearly done is pretty good." They'd been working on the village ever since Brian had told her the boxes were in his garage. It had been a great distraction from what was going on with Jay Turner, and she and Brian had been having so much fun. He'd even sacrificed his dining table so she had somewhere to set everything up.

"It usually takes me less than an hour to decorate my whole house for Christmas," Brian said.

"That's because you only have a tree with lights," she shot back, pointing to the Christmas tree in the corner of the room.

Brian shrugged. "Between work and volunteering I'm hardly ever here, and we always do Christmas Day at my parents' house, or one of my uncles, or your parents, so there doesn't seem much point in going all out."

"I live alone, and we never do Christmas at my house, and I still decorate every room."

"That's because you're Christmas crazy." Brian poked his tongue out at her.

She laughed again. They'd really had such a wonderful morning, and Brian had been so patient as she fiddled with each of the buildings trying to decide how they would best fit onto the table. At her house, she had the village spread out over a specially designed two-tier table her dad had made for her when she first moved into her own place.

Once she'd spread out the roll of cotton wool, she had to arrange the pine trees, snow-lined road, bridge, and stream pieces. Then she had to set out the thirty buildings, including an array of shops, an elf toy factory, an elf workshop, reindeer grooming cottage, reindeer flying school, a cottage for Santa and Mrs. Claus, a countdown clock tower, Mrs. Claus kitchen, North Pole observatory, and the Santa's Workshop that had been her very first Lemax Christmas Village piece. Then there were the trains, campfires, cocoa bars, North Pole mailbox, signs, candy cane swings, lampposts, ponds for ice skating, sleighs, sleds, winter animals, reindeer, elves, Christmas trees, and people.

"Just how many Christmas trees do you have?" Brian asked as he unpacked another from the boxes.

She scanned the table. "I have ten, and that one is the last."

"Finally." He sighed dramatically.

Hayley playfully punched him in the shoulder. They were such good friends it was hard to think of doing anything that might ruin that. And yet whenever they were together like this, enjoying one another's company, it was hard not to want more. If they were a couple, they could spend the rest of their lives like this, laughing, teasing each other, and having fun.

Some days she almost felt like it was wrong to want more than she had. After everything she had been through and how her life could have turned out, having parents she adored, a little sister she loved, friends and extended family who she knew would do anything for her, it seemed greedy to ask for anything else.

And yet ...

She couldn't help it.

She *did* want more.

She wanted Brian.

"So, uh, where do you think it should go?" she asked, suddenly self-conscious.

"I think there's a little space left between the Silent Night Stable and the Snow Day scene, just behind the Snowdad and Snowbaby on the bench."

"I think you're right," she agreed. "If I move the costumed canines and the carolers over a tiny bit this last tree should fit."

"Here you go." He handed her the tree.

As she reached to take the Christmas tree her fingers brushed against Brian's. Her heart fluttered in her chest, her stomach flip-flopped, and of their own accord her lips parted, her tongue darting out to wet them.

Quickly, she grabbed the tree and set it in place, then stood back to admire the village. It was a lot more crowded than usual, but it still looked beautiful and Christmassy. It wasn't just the fact that the Christmas village was pretty and got her in the Christmas spirit that made her love it. It was that every single piece had been a gift from someone she loved. Every year her parents gave her a new piece, starting with the Santa's Workshop they'd given her the first Christmas she spent with them. Other family and friends had joined in when she started seriously collecting them around the age of ten, and it had quickly become her own special Christmas tradition.

"So, how do you think it looks?" Hayley asked, admiring their handiwork.

"Adorable."

"It's more crowded than I usually do it. Usually, I have Santa's Wonderland altogether on the top layer of the table and the village together on the bottom. But I think you can still see everything." She stepped back up to the table and slightly rearranged a kissing Santa and Mrs. Claus.

"It looks great, Hales," Brian assured her, slipping an arm around her shoulders and drawing her close.

She stiffened as her body touched his.

Being this close was sweet torture. She found herself wishing that there weren't clothes between them. His naked body against hers and their hands exploring each other's bodies. Hayley couldn't help but shiver, she didn't usually think things like this, but then again, she and Brian weren't usually alone together like this. Usually when they hung out it was with their families.

Brian cleared his throat and shifted his body, angling it slightly away from her, and she wondered whether it was to try to hide that he was thinking about the two of them together just like she was.

"Thanks for helping me," she said, trying to break the tension that was starting to fill the room.

"Anytime." Brian's voice had gone husky, and even though she wasn't looking at him she knew that he was staring at her the same way he had in her house yesterday when he came to check on her.

Why did he keep looking at her like he wanted to kiss her?

She wished he would just tell her if that was what he was thinking. Or that she could find enough courage to tell him how she felt.

"Hayley," Brian started, but was interrupted when the doorbell rang. He sighed, then said, "I better get that."

She watched him cross the room, wondering what he had been about to say to her. Turning back to the village, she wanted to believe that he'd been going to say that he had feelings for her, and to ask her out on a date, but she was pretty sure that was only wishful thinking.

"It's Sophie," Brian announced, coming back to join her.

"Oh, your Christmas village survived the fire," Sophie exclaimed, giving her a hug. "I'm so glad."

"Thankfully most of my stuff survived. He didn't use an accelerant, so the fire burned the carpets and floorboards where the rocks landed. One landed on my bed too, and my mannequin was destroyed, but other than that everything else was okay," she explained.

"I'm just glad *you're* okay." Sophie gave her another hug.

"You all finished here?" Brian asked. "Can I pack away the boxes?"

"We're done except for the fake snow. I usually make some up and then sprinkle it about everywhere."

"Why don't you and Sophie go and talk, and I'll do that."

"Okay, thanks." She smiled at him, but he was back to the brisk

Brian that had been here last night. The relaxed guy she had been hanging out with for the last several hours had disappeared. Hayley wasn't used to Brian behaving like this, it was disconcerting.

"I brought sandwiches from your favorite café," Sophie told her as they went and sat on one of the couches. "Too bad I didn't bring a knife."

"Huh?" she asked as she took one of the sandwiches.

"To cut the tension."

"What tension?"

"Between you and Brian. Are you blind? Don't you see it? The way he looks at you, I think he's way more interested in you than you think he is. And didn't we have a deal? We were both going to try to put our messed-up pasts behind us and move on. Weren't you supposed to talk to Brian, tell him how you felt?"

Deal or no deal she just wasn't sure she could do it. Every time she thought about telling him she backed out. It was like she was physically incapable. The words got stuck in her throat and refused to come out. "I don't think now is the best time to be getting into that. Brian is my bodyguard, and I'm stuck here until Jay Turner is caught. If I tell him and he turns me down, it's going to make things pretty awkward."

"I don't think stuck is quite the right word to use for you staying at Brian's house," Sophie contradicted. "You should use this time to your advantage. It's just the two of you here, no distractions, nothing to do but hang out together. From the looks of things, he spent all morning helping you set up your village, he wouldn't have done that if he didn't like you. And there has to be some perks to living here rather than just hanging out. I mean, he might walk around half-naked or something. I saw Brian when we had that pool party at the end of the summer, he works out a lot."

Immediately, her mind jumped back to this morning when Brian had come downstairs dressed in nothing but the sweatpants he slept in. He had a perfectly toned body, but she wasn't into that kind of thing. Well of course she was a woman, and she appreciated a well-toned, sculpted male specimen, but she didn't care about looks, she wanted someone who made her feel safe, special, and loved.

But she couldn't deny that Brian's sexy six-pack and toned arms had stirred up a pit of desire in her belly.

"He has been walking around half-naked, hasn't he?" Sophie grinned, no doubt noticing her bright pink cheeks. "I told you there were perks to living here." Then her friend grew serious. "There's nothing wrong with taking advantage of that, Hayley. Not Brian being half-naked, I mean, being here with him. It is the perfect chance for him to realize that you two belong together. Don't waste it, okay?"

5:26 P.M.

A waste of a day.

Jay hadn't been able to find where Hayley Hood was hiding out, and he couldn't go back home. As far as he knew his kid was still in a foster home, and he didn't know where his wife was or what she was doing.

At least he had found a place he could hide out for a while.

Tilting his head back he drank half the can of beer in one long gulp then threw it away, letting it join the others on the floor.

Right now, he didn't have a long-term plan.

Kill the social worker was a given. And get his kid back. But he hadn't thought any further ahead than that. He supposed he'd take his wife and daughter and leave town. If he was on the run, he wouldn't be able to keep collecting welfare, but there were other ways to make money. He could always get his wife to prostitute herself, or there were people out there who would pay good money for a pretty little girl. His kid had betrayed him after all, and he really had no use for a child. At least that way he could make a little cash.

He picked up another can and opened it, downing most of it in one go. He'd been drinking for the last hour now, a dozen empty cans lay scattered on the floor. It probably wasn't the smartest way to spend his time when he had someone he was hunting, but it sure beat just sitting here getting angrier by the second.

He wanted to find Hayley.

He wanted her writhing, screaming body lying beneath him while he made her pay for messing with his life.

How hard could it be to find one woman?

She had to be somewhere, it wasn't like she had just disappeared, she was hiding, but like all hiding animals she would eventually come creeping back into the light. And he had a pretty good idea where she would end up when she did. All he had to do was wait long enough, and he'd get his hands on her.

His hand curled around the can he clutched, crushing it, and imagining it was Hayley's neck. Beer sloshed over it, and he sucked it off. Maybe he'd have a little fun with Hayley Hood before he tortured and killed her.

"J-Jay?"

He startled at the sound of the voice, lurching to his feet so quickly his chair toppled over, clattering loudly against the linoleum floor. As he turned around a smile—or more accurately a snarl—curled his lips.

"Hello, Maria," he said slowly. It looked like his day was going to pick up a little after all.

"I-I came as-as quickly as I could," his wife stammered, her gaze fixed firmly on the floor. It hadn't taken long to teach her that a woman should never look her husband in the eye unless she was asked to.

His father had taught his mother that same lesson.

Jay was three the first time he remembered hearing the sound of flesh slapping flesh.

That thwack as a hand connected with a cheek or a bare backside.

The way blood bubbled up at the corner of someone's mouth when knuckles slammed into a delicate face.

The way tears seemed to hover perilously before slowly sliding down a pale cheek stained red with a handprint.

Those things had been his introduction to life.

It wasn't just his mother that his father used to like to beat up on. His older brother used to get the brunt of their dad's anger before he grew bigger than their dad and the cowardly old man turned his attention on his daughter. His sister had been a pretty girl before their father smashed her face into a mirror when she screamed while he was raping her. After that, her face looked more like a jigsaw puzzle than the face of a thirteen-year-old girl.

With a son he was too scared to lay a hand on, and a daughter he no longer found beautiful enough to head to her room when he was drunk after dinner, his father had no one else to turn his violent temper onto but Jay.

On a good day, he was lucky to just get a belt to the back of the legs.

On a bad day, he might be locked outside in the snow, given nothing to eat, be beaten so badly he couldn't get out of bed to go to school the following day.

But time was on his side and not on his father's. He grew bigger, taller, and stronger while his father—crippled by a lifetime of alcohol abuse—grew weaker. The day he turned fifteen he realized that he was now bigger than his father, and when the man attempted to swing a fist into the side of his head, he blocked it and then shoved the man so hard he went right through the kitchen window.

After that, his father kept his temper focused solely on his wife.

Jay felt no pity for the woman. She had done nothing to try to leave the man who beat her senseless, and who abused all three of her children. She deserved everything she got. If she couldn't keep her house and herself and her children the way her husband wanted then she should have been beaten.

His mother had failed as a wife and mother.

His wife wasn't doing any better.

"Come here," he ordered.

Maria's eyes darted up, met his, clearly conveyed her panic, then dropped back to the floor, and she walked the ten feet to the table.

"Where is Kinsley?"

"She-she's still in-in the foster home," she whispered, her voice barely audible.

"Why didn't you get her back?"

"Th-they said that-that they couldn't be sure that-that I wasn't involved in-in what happened to-to Leah," she stammered. Her eyes grew watery at the mention of their oldest daughter. She was grieving, but Jay didn't care that the teenager was dead, he just wished that he had been able to teach her to mind her mouth when she was in his presence.

"What are you going to do to get her back?"

"I-I-I don't think I can."

"That seems to be a habit of yours, doesn't it? You couldn't get Leah to shut that sassy mouth. You couldn't get Kinsley to shut her mouth either. Now you're letting strangers keep our kid. Strip."

Once again Maria's blue eyes flew to his, begging him not to do what she already knew he had made up his mind to do.

Disobeying him now was not a smart move.

He was already so angry he was ready to explode and the only one here to take the brunt of that anger was his wife.

She knew better than to provoke him when he was like this.

"Strip," he repeated, over-enunciating the word.

With visibly shaking hands, Maria did as she was told. She pulled her sweater over her head and folded it neatly, setting it down on the table because she knew how he hated clothes lying on the floor. Her jeans joined the sweater as did a pair of socks, a bra, and panties.

Maria stood naked before him, trembling in the cold room, but he knew it wasn't because of the temperature, it was because of fear. The knowledge turned him on and made him grow hard.

Jay walked around his wife. Her arms remained straight at her sides; she knew he hated when she tried to cover herself in his presence. Her body was thin and a little bony in places. Her pale skin was marred with a litany of scars and a couple of fresher, partially healed gashes. Each mark was a sign of his power, authority, and his strength.

He sat back down in the chair he'd been in before his wife had arrived. "Come," he told her.

Further instruction wasn't needed. Maria came and draped herself over his lap, her bare backside screaming out to him.

With one hand he unbuckled his belt, with his other he slapped her, pleased when the white skin immediately tinted pink. He hit her again, and then again, then as he slid his belt free it replaced his hand, and he hit her half a dozen more times until small welts began to appear.

Adrenalin flooded his system, and spurred on by the bloody welts, he reigned down a bevy of strikes until he could feel Maria's body shuddering as she wept silently. Picking up his wife's small body he tossed her down to the floor. When he stood above her, he had never felt so powerful in his life.

Swinging his leg back, he rammed it into Maria's ribs, imagining it was Hayley Hood who lay powerless and helpless at his feet.

Soon it would be.

But for now, his wife would have to suffice.

~

6:12 P.M.

Jessica Spears knew that everyone had different life experiences and that shaped the way they looked at the world. But as she looked through the window at Maria Turner, who was lying on a hospital bed, she couldn't understand how a woman would go back to a man who hurt her so badly now that she had a chance to be free.

Maria had been found passed out on the sidewalk, beaten so badly she had collapsed. It didn't take a detective to figure out that she had been to see her husband.

Jessica had worked enough domestic violence cases to know that a lot of factors played into why those women stayed. She would never judge anyone for their choices and how their lives turned out.

After all, she hadn't made the best decisions in her life.

Married a month after graduating high school to an older man who moved into the house next door to where her family lived. For her, it had been love at first sight, and ignoring the warnings of her family and friends, they were married only six weeks after they met.

Pregnant at nineteen.

Freddie was born when she was twenty.

Divorced by twenty-one.

It had been a whirlwind three and a half years and the roughest time in her life. Her husband might not have physically abused her, but he was controlling and emotionally manipulative and had cheated on her repeatedly.

The whole thing had been a learning experience, and she had

learned that relationships just weren't worth it. Jessica just wanted to focus on being the best mother to her five-year-old son that she could be. With how she behaved regarding her husband and ignoring her family's warnings, she had burned some bridges and although her family were still a part of her and Freddie's lives, she wasn't comfortable asking them to help. Since her husband had let her keep the house in the divorce, she was able to have a nanny who cared for Freddie before and after school, so she didn't have to rely on family. The rest of the time it was just the two of them, except for the weekends when Adam had Freddie and the ones where she had Claire.

Her life could be better, but in the end, she was happy, and her son was happy, and that was what mattered.

Jessica hoped that one day Maria and her daughter Kinsley could be happy as well. Maybe once Jay was in prison the two of them could have a fresh start. They'd definitely have a better life, they'd both be safe and no longer in danger of being beaten or murdered.

"Think she'll talk to us?" Adam asked, coming up beside her. They'd already gone home for the day when they got the call that Maria Turner had been spotted collapsing on the sidewalk and rushed to the hospital. Jessica had already sent the nanny home, so she'd had no choice but to call her parents and ask them to watch Freddie. They always seemed happy to do it, she knew they loved their grandson, but she still felt uncomfortable asking for their help.

"I want to say yes, but honestly, no I don't think she's going to tell us where her husband is hiding out. She's had plenty of opportunities to do the right thing. If she didn't turn him in for killing her daughter then she's not going to do it for trying to kill a social worker."

"I hate to say it, but I agree with you."

Despite them both feeling like this was pointless, they headed into the hospital room. Maria had a broken cheekbone, arm, cracked ribs, and bruises all over her body. Although they weren't visible, Jessica also knew that there were welts on the woman's backside, back, and the backs of her thighs from being hit repeatedly with a belt.

Maria didn't turn toward them when they entered the room, nor did she open her eyes, but from the small, hitched breath and sigh, Jessica knew that the woman was awake and aware of their presence.

"Mrs. Turner, it's Detective Spears and Detective Abram," Jessica said, drawing a chair over to the bed and taking a seat. Adam stood on the other side of the bed so Maria couldn't ignore them. "We know it was your husband who did this to you. You know where he's hiding out, we need you to tell us where he is so we can arrest him."

The woman cracked open one swollen eye, the other was swollen completely shut, but she remained stubbornly silent.

"He killed your daughter," Adam reminded her. "Even if that's not enough to get you to turn him in, you know he's a danger not just to you, but to your other daughter."

"Kinsley is all you have left," Jessica continued. "What happens if you get her back? Are you going to let Jay near her again? Are you going to risk letting him kill her as well?"

"He's her father," Maria croaked through her split lips.

"That doesn't give him the right to hurt her," Adam said, indignant. She knew that this case was getting to him. As a single father devoted to his daughter, he hated that there were men out there who abused their children.

It was clear from the expression on her bruised and battered face that Maria Turner disagreed with them. Years of being abused and told she was worth nothing had convinced her that it was true. Jessica didn't think they were going to be able to convince the woman otherwise, at least not yet, but maybe if they approached this from a different angle they might have better luck.

"Your husband tried to murder Hayley Hood," she told Maria.

The woman's face remained blank for a moment, then she nodded and murmured, "The social worker."

"That's right. Jay Turner managed to find where Hayley lived and set her house on fire with her inside it." She and Hayley were close in age and were quite friendly, not that Jessica had much time for friends, being a single mom with a demanding job was tough.

"She took Kinsley away from us," Maria said.

"She did her job," Adam corrected. "And you could have prevented Kinsley from being removed from your care. If you had backed up her story that Jay was on the roof when Leah fell to her death, he would have been arrested, and you'd still have your daughter."

From the horrified look in her blue eyes, that idea terrified the woman.

Terror rolled off Maria in waves. It was almost palpable, filling up the room. She was too scared of what Jay would do to her if she disobeyed him. And from the injuries he had inflicted on her tonight, she had every reason to be afraid. Jay had beaten her, and so far, she hadn't done anything to him. She had stood by him, even though it had cost her both her children.

"Hayley Hood doesn't deserve to be hurt or killed just for doing her job," Jessica said. "She's trying to protect Kinsley, keep her safe. Kinsley doesn't deserve to be hurt by her father anymore. Leah didn't deserve what her father did to her. Don't stand by and let him do the same thing to Kinsley. Maria," she paused and waited until the other woman was looking at her, "*you* don't deserve what Jay has done to you. You didn't deserve this." She waved her hands at the woman's injuries. "I know you loved Leah and I know that you love Kinsley. We're asking you to do the right thing for yourself and your daughter. Honor Leah's memory by keeping her little sister safe. The two of you deserve to be happy and safe. I know deep down inside that's what you want for yourself and your little girl. We know you know where your husband is hiding, you were with him tonight. Please do the right thing and tell us where to find him so that no one else gets hurt."

A single tear welled up in Maria's good eye and wound a slow path down her black and blue cheek.

Jessica prayed that what she'd said had gotten through. That Maria would realize that she deserved better than what her husband was giving her, that she was worth something, and so was her daughter.

"I can't turn Jay in. He's my husband, I promised to honor and obey him," Maria said, then closed her eyes, shutting them out.

She sighed, disappointed, she'd thought she was so close to getting through to her. But with or without Maria Turner's help, they were going to find Jay, and when they did, he would spend the rest of his life in prison.

~

8:53 P.M.

"Want some more hot chocolate?"

"Sure, thanks," Brian said, passing his mug to Hayley, then watching her as she walked to the kitchen. Her long dark hair hung all the way to her bottom, and when she wore it loose like she was right now it swung slightly from side to side as she moved. He'd known her since she was five years old and she had never colored it, not that there was anything wrong with dying your hair, but he liked that Hayley didn't. She was natural, she was real, beautiful inside and out. A kind, compassionate, and empathetic woman. It wasn't an act. She wasn't trying to impress anyone, it was just who she was, and he loved that about her.

He liked her.

*Liked* liked her.

Thought that the two of them might actually make a good couple kind of liked.

In the back of his mind, there had always been an attraction there, Hayley was beautiful with her long dark hair, pale skin, and large, long-lashed blue eyes, but he'd always been afraid that the six-year age gap was too much. Seeing how she had handled what had happened last night with such calm and grace, not panicking, just doing what had to be done, and making the best of the situation in the aftermath of the fire, including being forced to live with a bodyguard, he knew that the age gap was meaningless.

Coming so close to losing her had made him realize that his feelings ran deeper than just attraction. You couldn't build a relationship on mere physical attraction to your partner, not a lasting one anyway, and he wanted a relationship like his parents and his grandparents had. He wanted one where in old age you were still happy and excited to have your partner sitting by your side.

He wanted that with Hayley.

Those feelings of attraction were growing into something more, something real and strong, the more time he spent with her.

"I put a little grated chocolate on top," Hayley said, joining him back on the couch and passing him his mug.

A smile spread over his face as he looked at the mug of hot chocolate. "Remember that camping trip our families took together, the one when you were twelve?"

Hayley rolled her eyes at him, but a smile tugged at the corners of her mouth. "Must you bring that up every time we drink hot chocolate?"

"Come on, it's a funny story." He laughed.

"To you maybe," she shot back.

"I'll never forget the look on your face." He laughed again. "There we all were sitting around the campfire, making S'mores and drinking hot chocolate, laughing and talking and telling ghost stories. Then Tony jumps out from behind the trees, dressed in that hockey mask, with the fake machete, and you scream and stand up so quickly you spilled your hot chocolate all over yourself and knocked your chair into the fire."

"Your brother thought he was so funny. And I don't remember any of you being any help, you just all laughed, and there I am soaked in hot chocolate. It was cold that night, and those were the only clothes I had. I had to sleep in them still all wet." All he could do was laugh, and Hayley poked her tongue out at him. "I wouldn't be all smug, I seem to remember a certain someone making a fool of themselves when a certain spider startled them."

"Hey, spiders are disgusting." Brian shuddered at the mere mention of the beasts.

"So are scary movies. I hated those Friday the 13th movies, but Sophie was going through a horror movie phase and made me watch them with her. We were camping down by a lake, and it was Friday the 13th when Tony came out of the woods for a moment I thought he was Jason Voorhees. But at least that was over something scary. What about you scrambling out of your sleeping bag so fast you made the whole tent collapse, and all over the tiniest of spiders."

"That thing was huge," he contradicted. "And I didn't make the whole tent collapse."

Hayley giggled. "Oh, yes you did. And that scream was loud enough to wake the dead."

"I'd like to see what you'd do if you're lying there going to sleep and a spider the size of your hand starts crawling all over you."

"The size of your hand?" Hayley scoffed. "It was about this big." She held her hand up, her thumb and forefinger about a quarter of an inch apart.

"Try this." He reached over and put his own thumb and forefinger between hers, pushing them apart until they were as stretched out and far away from each other as it was possible to be.

"Those were fun times, all of us together, out in the woods, swimming in the lake, sitting around the campfire. We used to laugh so much."

"I miss those days," he said a little wistfully. Growing up he'd had so much fun with his siblings, cousins, and family friends. He still did, but things were different now. Both his younger sisters were married, and all his cousins were either dating or involved or busy with their jobs. Even his little baby cousin was eight years old now, no longer a baby, no one hung like they used to anymore.

"Yeah, me too. But nothing stays the same forever, which isn't always a bad thing. If my mom and your uncles hadn't found me then I'd still be a prisoner in Malachi's house. Sometimes change doesn't always seem so good at first, like right now, reminiscing about the fun we used to have is making us miss those days, but one day we're going to be back in the woods with our parents and all of our kids. Watching them swim in the lake, fish, swing on the rope out into the water, and sit around the campfire at night trying to scare each other with their ghost stories, just like our parents watched us."

She was right.

Change didn't have to be a bad thing, and one day when they were all married with kids of their own, he was sure those camping trips to the woods would start up again.

"When did you get to be so smart?"

She gave him a one-sided smile. "I guess when you've been through something traumatic like I have you either learn to look at the positives in life or the negatives will crush you. Like you, after you beat leukemia when you were a kid, you could have let it shape your life for the worse, but it didn't, it made you want to help people. That's why you became a doctor, right?"

"Right." He'd known he wanted to be a doctor for as long as he could remember. He'd only been a very small boy when he was diagnosed with leukemia, and while he didn't remember a lot from those years, what he did remember was being afraid of dying. At five years old he hadn't really understood what death was, but he had known that it was leaving behind his family, and he had known that his parents would be devastated and never fully heal.

That wasn't the only time he had thought he was going to die. When he was sixteen, he had started feeling really tired, losing weight, getting frequent infections, having nosebleeds, and bruising easily. Afraid that his leukemia was coming back he had gone to see his doctor but hadn't told his parents, who were having problems at the time, which he hadn't wanted to add to. Instead, he had let his fear turn to anger, and he'd lashed out at his mother, something he still wasn't proud of.

He had let his fear get the best of him.

Is that what he was doing now with Hayley?

Was he letting the fear that they might try being together and it wouldn't work out, and he'd lose one of his best friends stop him from even trying anything with her?

He wanted a wife and a family, and he was sure that Hayley wanted the same things. He had fun with her, they were great friends and had been for most of their lives. They made each other happy, and bottom line was, he thought he was falling in love with her.

Or maybe he had been in love with her all along, he wasn't sure, but he was sure that now wasn't the right time for them to be starting a relationship. Once Jay Turner was in custody and he wasn't responsible for keeping Hayley alive, they could sit down and talk.

"What are you thinking about?" Hayley asked.

Brian looked at her, at those soulful blue eyes, and he knew he couldn't wait. Bad timing or not, he had to tell Hayley he was falling for her.

No matter what happened he was sure that nothing could ruin their friendship. Not if both of them were determined not to let that happen.

"Well, I'm going to go to bed," Hayley announced when he didn't immediately answer her question. "I didn't sleep last night, and it's finally catching up with me. Thanks for hanging out with me today, I really appreciate it, you really helped keep my mind off what's going on." She leaned over and kissed his cheek, then carried her mug to the kitchen, rinsed it out, and put it in the dishwasher, then paused at the bottom of the stairs. "Goodnight, Brian."

"Yeah, night," he echoed as she walked upstairs. He lifted his hand and touched it to his cheek where she had kissed him. There was no longer any doubt about it, he wasn't developing feelings for Hayley, he already had them, and they were growing stronger by the second. He didn't think waiting until this was over was an option.

# CHAPTER
## *Three*

December 21st
9:05 A.M.

"I don't think this is a good idea."

"Haven't we argued about this enough already this morning?" Hayley asked, looking sideways at Brian, who was driving the car.

Argue had been pretty much all they had done since they got up this morning. Brian had already been up, showered, and dressed by the time she got up at seven o'clock. As soon as she was showered and dressed, she'd asked him to take her to see Kinsley Turner. The little girl hadn't been very forthcoming with any of the adults who had tried to get her to open up, and she thought she might have better luck because she understood what it was like to be five years old and escape the clutches of a monster, but still be terrified about what was going to happen to you.

While she thought it was a good idea, Brian disagreed.

Vehemently.

He thought it was too dangerous, but Hayley thought that as long as he was with her, Jay Turner wasn't going to be stupid enough to try coming after her again.

Besides, as far as they knew Jay was already long gone. Yes, he wanted her dead, but more than that he wanted to be in control, and going to prison was one of the worst things that could happen to a control freak. If it came down to a choice between getting his revenge on her or self-preservation, Hayley believed that he was going to choose self-preservation every time.

"We didn't argue, we discussed," Brian said tightly.

She huffed a mirthless laugh. "I don't think using the words, 'I forbid you to leave this house until Jay Turner is in custody' can be construed as a discussion."

"I didn't say forbid." He huffed.

She laughed again, more genuinely this time. "You totally did."

One side of his mouth curved up. "Okay, so maybe I shouldn't have said it like that, but I'm just worried about you, Hayley. When you called me, trapped inside your house, with that man throwing rocks roused in fire through your window, I'd never been so scared in my life. I don't want anything like that to happen ever again."

It was hard to argue with that sentiment.

And she supposed it was kind of sweet. Not the attempting to forbid her to do something thing, but that he cared enough about her to worry like that. She knew it went deeper than him just being her body-guard. They'd been friends for so many years that this wasn't just a job to him.

"I don't want that to happen again either," she told Brian. "But you're not going to let Jay hurt me."

"No, I won't," Brian vowed. There was something in his tone, it sounded a little like the way her dad talked to her mom. That air of protectiveness that you had when you cared about someone so deeply that even the thought of something or someone hurting them hurt you too.

Hayley had no idea what was going on with Brian. Last night when they'd been reminiscing about the past, he'd been looking at her with that weird expression on his face again. She still wanted to believe it was because he was finally seeing her as something other than just a friend, but she was also cautious about getting her hopes up too high.

"We're here," Brian announced, and her attention snapped immediately from wishing that her feelings for him were reciprocated to where she was and why they were here.

"I hope this works. I hope I can get through to her," she said, more to herself than Brian.

"You will," he said confidently.

She wished she had the same faith in herself as Brian. Usually, she was pretty good at getting the children she worked with to open up to her, it was like they sensed she understood what they were going through. But Kinsley was different because Kinsley had seen her father attack her sister and knew—as young as she was—just how dangerous her dad could be.

"Wait in the car until I come around," Brian told her. "And then stay close as we walk to the door. I'll stay just a step behind you just in case Jay Turner is here and decides to try anything."

Hayley had to fight against her natural inclination to object to being so closely monitored. It wasn't since she was a very little girl that someone else had watched over her like this and it felt odd, even if it was Brian and she was hopelessly in love with him.

But Jay really could be out there somewhere.

And he really might take advantage of this opportunity to come after her again.

So, she nodded her assent and waited semi-patiently while Brian got out, walked around to her door, opened it for her, and shielded her body with his own as she climbed out. Hayley didn't really like the idea of Brian putting himself between her and potential danger. She didn't want him to get hurt because of her. She knew it was his job and that he was well trained, but she didn't know how she would live with herself if Jay hurt—or even worse—killed him in an attempt to get at her.

The walk to the door was uneventful, and Hayley punched in the code then slid her key into the lock and let them both inside. The group home where Kinsley was staying before she was placed with a family was a large one. Several dozen children lived here at any one time, from newborn babies to teenagers soon to age out of the system. The place was well run, the children were well taken care of, and the staff was wonderful, attempting to make the kids feel cared about and not just doing their jobs and making sure their physical needs were attended to.

"I'll go see where Kinsley's room is," she told Brian and headed for the desk in the foyer to press the buzzer. Although this was a home with so many people coming and going, social workers, therapists, doctors and nurses, and often police officers as well, there was a reception desk that was usually manned so that visitors could be directed to the correct room.

Brian trailed after her, and less than a minute after ringing the bell a harried woman appeared from the next room.

"Oh, Hayley," she said, smiling when she saw them. "I heard a little girl's father in one of your cases assaulted you."

"He did. And he made it clear he's not done with me yet. This is Brian Xander, he's my bodyguard until the man is in custody." Xander was a well-known last name in these circles since the Xander family and her own had been in law enforcement for many years as well as running a center for abused women and children, and from the look in the woman's eyes it clicked with her, and she smiled at Brian.

"Who are you here to see?"

"Kinsley Turner."

The woman checked a computer, then said, "She's staying in room 212, but she might be in the playroom."

"Thanks," she said to the woman, then to Brian, "let's check her room first."

If she had been brought to a place like this after she and her sisters had been rescued instead of going home with her adoptive parents, she wouldn't have felt comfortable around other children. While she and Kinsley had had very different experiences, she suspected the child would feel the same way.

When they walked into room 212 they did indeed find Kinsley Turner. The little girl was curled up on one of the bunk beds—there were four in the room—with a pile of books.

"Hey, Kinsley." She smiled, unsure how she would be received by the child.

The little girl looked up, recognition flashed through her blue eyes, and a small smile lit her lips. She reached behind the pile of books and pulled out the brown teddy bear she'd given her the day she had removed Kinsley from her home.

"Oh, you still have Brownie." She smiled and went to sit beside the girl. That Kinsley had kept the teddy bear had to be a good sign. "How does he like it here?"

"It's okay," Kinsley said slowly. "But I miss my house, and I miss my toys, and I miss Leah. The dark is scary, and Leah used to sing me a song when I got scared."

"Well, you know what you do, when you get scared, you hold onto Brownie real tight and you remember when you and your sister used to bake brownies, okay?"

"Okay," Kinsley agreed, her little face so serious.

In a way it was like looking in a mirror. When she was a little girl, she'd had the same serious, grown-up eyes that Kinsley did. The kind of eyes a child could only have when they lived through something no one —especially a little kid—should ever have to.

"When am I going to go home?" Kinsley asked.

Resisting the urge to just reassure the child, Kinsley needed honesty right now if she was going to survive the next few months. "I don't know, honey. You might go back home, but you might not. If you don't, you'll probably stay here for a while and then maybe go and live with a nice family." Hayley prayed it would be a nice family. If Kinsley couldn't return home to her mother, she prayed that the child would be adopted by a wonderful family just like she and Arianna had been.

She couldn't ask Kinsley any questions about Leah and her death because without a cop or a child advocate present anything that Kinsley told her could be considered inadmissible in court, but she could hang out here for a while, maybe read some stories, or play a game. It wasn't like she had anything else to do, she couldn't go to work until this situation with Kinsley's father was resolved, and she felt an affinity with the child because their early life experiences were so similar. Kinsley was the same age that she had been when she was rescued and adopted.

"You want to play for a while?" Hayley asked Kinsley.

The little girl smiled up at her. "Can you read to me?"

"I sure can." As she stretched out onto the bed, resting back against the wall, just able to sit up under the top bunk, Kinsley immediately curled up at her side. She really hoped that the sweet little girl was lucky enough to end up with a family who would love and care for her like she deserved.

~

10:44 A.M.

"And I heard him exclaim as he drove out of sight, merry Christmas to all, and to all a good night," Hayley read the last line of T'was the Night Before Christmas and set the book down.

For the last almost two hours, he and Hayley had been playing with Kinsley Turner. They'd read books, played dolls, built a tower out of Lego, played go fish, and snap. They'd giggled and talked and had fun. Hayley was a natural with little kids, she was going to make a great mom one day.

Brian loved kids too, he couldn't wait to have a child of his own. If he hadn't decided to go and work at his uncle's private security firm, he would probably have gone into pediatrics. When Elise had given birth to her daughter, he had been so excited to become an uncle to the first little Xander grandchild. Eve would soon be adding baby number two to their clan. He hoped it wouldn't be too much longer before he wasn't just Uncle Brian, but Dad Brian too.

"Can we read another story?" Kinsley asked.

He knew that Hayley would have said yes, but the longer she was out in the open the more she was in danger. Kinsley was at a group home. Maria Turner no doubt knew that her daughter was here, and since they knew she had been with her husband since Kinsley had been removed from their care there was every chance that Jay knew where his daughter was.

Which was why he hadn't wanted to come.

Brian knew they shouldn't be here, he knew that he was failing at his job as Hayley's bodyguard. If it was any other client they wouldn't be here, he would have put his foot down and said a definitive no.

But this wasn't any other client.

This was Hayley.

And when she had said that she had to come because she needed to make sure that the little girl was okay after everything she had been through, he just couldn't say no.

He just hoped that this wasn't going to wind up being a mistake.

It was time to go back home and get Hayley where he knew she was safe.

"Actually, honey," he said to the little girl, "we have to go now."

"Oh." Kinsley's face fell. "Can we play a game of Hungry Hippos before you go?"

Hayley looked to him, seeking his approval but he shook his head. He'd let her convince him to bring her here, but now it was time to do his job and take her home.

"I don't think so, honey," Hayley said.

"Are you going to come back?" It was clear in the last two hours Kinsley had become attached to Hayley. He wasn't sure that was a good idea.

"Of course I will," Hayley assured the child.

"Oh, goodie." Kinsley grinned and threw her arms around Hayley's neck, hugging her hard. "When are you coming back? Tomorrow?"

"I'm not sure, but I will definitely come back, and next time I'm going to beat you in snap and go fish."

Kinsley giggled. "I always used to beat Leah when we played games, I'm good at them."

"You sure are. Okay, Kinsley, we'll see you later. Why don't we walk you down to the playroom and you can beat some of the other kids," Hayley suggested.

"I want to stay here. Brownie and I want to read some more."

"All right, see you later," Hayley said the words but the look on her face clearly said she didn't want to leave. If he let her, she would probably spend the whole day here with Kinsley Turner. But right now, it was his job to keep Hayley alive, and he wasn't comfortable having her here. He had been on edge ever since they stepped out his front door and he wouldn't relax until they were back inside his house.

"Bye, Hayley. Bye, Brian," Kinsley said, picking up the teddy bear

Hayley had given her and holding it tightly in her arms as she watched them leave.

They walked in silence back down the stairs and to the front door. "Stay behind me," he reminded her before they stepped outside.

"Mmhmm," Hayley said, it sounded non-committal, but he knew she would do it even though she didn't like it.

It wasn't until they were in the car and a couple of blocks down the road that he spoke again. "I don't think it's a good idea that you go back and see Kinsley again."

"What? Why?" Hayley demanded.

"Look how attached she was to you in just two hours. Once her father is found and in prison, she'll either go back to her mother or she'll be placed with a foster family. How is she going to cope if she's become reliant on you?" He didn't want to fight with Hayley, and he didn't want to make her feel bad because he knew that she genuinely cared about every child in every case she worked, but he didn't want to see her get too attached just like he didn't want to see Kinsley get too attached.

"When I look at her, I see me when I was five years old," Hayley said softly.

"I know you do." Brian reached over and took her hand, squeezing it tightly. "Are you thinking of what it would be like to be her mother?"

Hayley's eyes flew to his. "There is no evidence that Maria was involved in Leah's death, she'll no doubt get Kinsley back."

"But if she doesn't, if she enters the system, you want to take her."

"I just want her to have a good life. I want someone to save her, I want her to be happy, and part of me wants to pay forward what my parents did for me," Hayley admitted.

"I think that's amazing, and one day you're going to make such a difference in a child's life, but I'm not sure that child will be Kinsley, and I don't want to see you get hurt."

"I can't explain it, Brian, I just feel a connection to her. I've worked with so many kids since I became a social worker, and I care about all of them and want to do whatever I can for all of them to make their lives better, but with Kinsley, it just feels different."

"Maybe it's because she's the same age as you were when you were saved, and she does look like you, with the dark hair and the blue eyes.

Maybe that's why you're identifying with her so—" his sentence was cut off when their car was rammed from behind.

It was snowing out, lightly, but if you weren't used to driving in snow it could be a little disconcerting, and for a moment, he thought it was just an inexperienced driver losing control and hitting their car.

But then they were hit again.

"Brian." Hayley squeezed the hand that still held hers.

"Hold on." He quickly squeezed back then put both hands on the wheel as a third slam shook the car.

"It's Jay," Hayley said.

She was almost definitely right. "Maria must have told him where Kinsley was, and he knew that sooner or later you would turn up there so he was lying in wait."

"I'm sorry," Hayley apologized as she finally realized why he hadn't wanted to take her there.

He wanted to reassure her, but the car that had been hitting them from behind rushed up at their side, cutting them off and giving him no choice but to veer off the road.

Brian tugged on the wheel, intending to swerve around the car and get back in front, but as though anticipating that was what he would try to do, Jay sped up, and before he could do anything about it they slammed into a tree.

Hayley's side took the brunt of the impact, but his body was still flung forward and then jerked backward with a snap that was felt through every inch of his body.

A car door slammed.

Footsteps sounded.

His head was ringing, and the urge to check on Hayley was strong, but he ignored it and pulled out his gun.

"Don't move, Jay," he ordered. He couldn't really see where the man was, but he knew he was out there somewhere.

"I'm here for the girl," a voice snarled, and then Hayley's door handle jiggled.

Brian didn't think twice.

He aimed the gun and fired.

A frustrated growl let him know he hit his target, but the pounding footsteps and revving car engine said the wound he had inflicted wasn't serious enough to incapacitate Jay Turner.

Getting out of the car in time to get a license plate wasn't an option because his body was still pulsing with a steady beat of pain, and he knew he wasn't coordinated enough to move quickly yet.

Instead, he turned to Hayley who was slumped in her seat, blood streaking the side of her face.

Brian pressed his fingers to Hayley's neck, and she immediately stirred. "I'm all right, just sore. You got him."

"Not enough to stop him, I'm sorry." He knew he should have trusted his instincts and kept Hayley at his house whether she liked it or not.

Hayley winced but turned her head in his direction. "You stopped him from dragging me out of the car, don't be sorry, you just saved my life."

"I got you hurt." His gaze went to a gash on her forehead, and he gently grasped her chin, angled her face, and touched the tip of his finger to her temple.

"You saved my life," she repeated.

His heart was still racing, and he leaned over and rested his forehead on the top of Hayley's head. If Jay Turner had gotten his hands on her, he never would have forgiven himself. Brian couldn't imagine his life without Hayley in it—nor did he want to.

Right now, he had to get Hayley medical treatment and then someplace safe, then the two of them needed to talk.

11:01 A.M.

Brian rested his forehead against hers.

Despite the raging headache she had from bumping her head twice in as many days, the first thought that popped into her mind was that she hoped the next thing he did was kiss her.

But he didn't.

Someone hammered on the car door, and Brian released her and turned around.

"Are you okay?" someone demanded, yanking the driver's door open.

Brian put his gun away. "We're okay. Have the cops been called? And an ambulance?"

"I don't need an ambulance," Hayley protested automatically.

"We'll see," Brian shot over his shoulder.

"I called 911 when that other car ran you off the road," the woman at the car door said. "Did you know him?"

"Unfortunately, we did," Brian replied.

If there had been any doubt before that Jay Turner was determined to kill her then it was gone now. He wasn't going to stop until he got what he wanted. And what he wanted was her dead. Probably a long, drawn-out death.

"I better call your mom, Ryan, and Brady. We need to decide how we're proceeding next."

While Brian made the call, Hayley rested her head back against the headrest and closed her eyes. Although she had a headache it wasn't all that bad. She didn't feel dizzy or nauseous, so didn't think she had a concussion, and she wasn't sore anywhere else so didn't think she had any other injuries either. All she wanted was to go home and lie down for a while.

Well not home.

As long as Jay Turner was out there, she couldn't go back home.

And they probably couldn't go back to Brian's house either.

Hopefully, the woman who had knocked on the car door or someone else had seen something that would help Adam, Jessica, and the rest of the police department find where Jay Turner was hiding.

He obviously knew where Kinsley was since he must have followed them from there knowing that sooner or later she would show up there so he'd staked out the place. She hoped that he didn't decide to try to get to Kinsley. He thought of the little girl as his property, and he would no doubt make a play to get her back at some point.

"How're you doing?"

Hayley opened her eyes to see Brian crouching beside her open door. "Okay, I'm just tired, and my head hurts a little, but I don't need to go to the hospital."

"Let me take a look at you." He picked up her wrist, checked her pulse, and then shone a light in her eyes.

Knowing what he was going to ask she rattled off, "No dizziness, no nausea, just a headache."

"All right, no hospital." He smiled, setting her hand down in her lap. "A cop is going to drive us into the office. Brady, Ryan, and your mom will meet us there."

Before she could climb out of the car, Brian reached over and unclipped her seat belt, then scooped her up into his arms, carrying her to a nearby cruiser. He set her on the backseat then slid in beside her, wrapping an arm protectively around her shoulders and settling her close at his side.

Hayley didn't fight it. Snuggled in Brian's arms was exactly where she wanted to be right now. How close she had come to being in Jay Turner's clutches was starting to sink in. He had been just outside the car. He'd been trying to get in. If Brian hadn't fired his gun at him, he probably would have gotten her.

Brian had saved her life.

She was the one who had wanted to go to the group home to visit with Kinsley Turner because she just couldn't shake the need to be there for the little girl. She'd worked with a lot of kids, and she'd never felt a connection like this to one of them before.

Because of her, Brian could have been seriously hurt.

As could anyone else who had been on the road when Jay had tried —succeeded—in running them off the road.

What would she have done if Brian had been hurt because of her?

She would never have forgiven herself.

Although she tried to divert her mind before it could go there, her thoughts started to fill with scenarios of what Jay was going to do to her if he got her. She knew he wanted her to suffer, and she knew that Maria had gone to see him yesterday and he'd beaten her badly enough that she had collapsed on the side of the road. Is that what he was going to do to her? Or would it be something even worse?

There were a lot of ways to hurt someone.

In her years as a social worker, she had seen a lot of horrible things done to children, and at the shelter her mom helped to run, she had seen a lot worse.

Was she going to end up like that?

Beaten, shot, stabbed, strangled, raped, all of that could be in her future.

"Hayley."

She looked up to find Brian looking down at her, a concerned look on his face. "You were whimpering. Are you feeling worse?"

"No, I was just thinking about ..." she trailed off not wanting to worry Brian further.

"About what?"

Hayley sighed, she may as well admit it, Brian would probably figure it out anyway. "I was just thinking about what's going to happen if Jay gets to me."

Brian roughly grabbed her chin and forced her to look at him. "I don't want you to worry about that. I told you I wouldn't let that man hurt you and I won't. At least not again." His blue eyes clouded over, and he touched just beside the cut on her head from the car crash. "I'll clean this and see if it needs stitches when we get to the office."

She wanted to say something, but her throat seemed to have closed up. Every time Brian was this close to her, she couldn't think of anything else, he had even banished thoughts of what Jay would do to her.

They stared into each other's eyes and probably would have continued to do so but the cop driving them to the private security firm offices pulled to a stop.

"We're here," the cop announced.

"Thank you," Brian said a little distractedly. "You know the drill," he reminded her before he got out of the car.

The second Brian released her she felt cold, and her fears began to creep back in. It was like Brian wasn't just her bodyguard he was also the guard that kept all of her anxieties at bay.

Staying close beside Brian as soon as they entered the lobby her mother threw her arms around her. "Are you okay?" she demanded, scanning her from head to toe and zeroing in on the blood on her forehead.

"I'm fine," Hayley assured her mom.

"What happened?" Mom looked to Brian for an answer.

"We went to the group home to see Kinsley Turner. Maria must have told her husband where Kinsley was, and Jay must have thought that Hayley would show up there sooner or later, so he was staking out the place. He must have followed us, he ran us off the road, then he tried to take Hayley. I shot at him, and I'm pretty sure I hit him, but obviously not badly enough. He got back in his car and drove off," Brian summarized.

"She can't go back to Brian's house," Ryan Xander said as he and Brady Crowley stepped out of the lift and came to join them.

"I agree." Brian nodded a little too vehemently.

"She could come home," her mom said.

"I don't think so," Ryan said. "If Jay Turner is smart enough to know that Hayley would have to go to the group home and wait for her to turn up, then he's smart enough to research Hayley's family."

"So, what do you suggest?" her mom asked.

"We thought she'd stay in one of our safehouses," Brady replied. "Ryan and I already set it up. She and Brian can go straight there from here, we've had the place stocked with food and some clothes for the two of them. They can stay there till the cops have Jay Turner in custody."

It was weird having everyone talk about her like she wasn't here.

Her mom, Ryan, and Brady had all been cops, and although it had been years since they left the force they slipped so easily back into those roles.

Going to the safehouse was the safest thing to do, but it also meant that unless Jay was found quickly, she was going to have to spend Christmas without her family, just her and Brian. Hayley knew what Sophie would say, she'd say to take advantage of the situation, but she wasn't sure that she could do that. She wanted Brian but only if he wanted her too.

Right now, being treated like a helpless victim or how she would be spending the holidays weren't her biggest concerns. There was only one thing that was worrying her.

"What about Kinsley?" she asked. "I'm afraid that Jay is going to go after her." She couldn't stand the thought of anything happening to that sweet little girl.

"Thought of that already." Brady smiled at her.

"Sawyer is going to stay at the group home," Ryan told her.

So, Kinsley was safe, she knew that Sawyer wouldn't let Jay get to her.

Which just left her and Brian alone in a safehouse, just the two of them. Hayley didn't know whether to be excited or terrified.

~

1:27 P.M.

"I hope we get something out of her."

"So do I." Adam agreed wholeheartedly with his partner. "But we're asking a lot from a five-year-old little girl."

"Kids usually notice a whole lot more than we give them credit for, you know that as well as I do. Hopefully, Kinsley will know something, even something small that might give us an idea of where her father might be hiding out."

"If we don't get something from her then I don't know how we're going to find Jay Turner. He's not going to come back to the group home, he knows we'll have it staked out, and he knows that Hayley won't be back here until he's in custody. We're not going to get anything out of Maria. She's made it very clear that her loyalties lie with her husband and not with either of her daughters or with Hayley. We'll keep looking, but the city is too big, it's not likely we'll just stumble across him. Kinsley is our only realistic chance of finding him."

Adam didn't want to celebrate Christmas knowing that such a dangerous man was roaming free. Jay was a danger to Hayley, his daughter, and his wife, and the sooner he was safely behind bars the better.

Hayley was safely tucked away in a safehouse with Brian Xander, who he knew would gladly give his own life if it meant saving Hayley's. Sooner or later, Jay Turner wouldn't be able to resist taking back his child, so Sawyer Watson would be the little girl's shadow until her father was caught.

Everyone was safe.

For now.

But he wanted Hayley and Brian to be able to celebrate Christmas with their families, not locked away someplace alone. Although he wasn't sure the two would mind the extra time together.

Neither he nor Jessica knew where they were. The only ones who knew were Ryan Xander and Brady Crowley who had arranged which safehouse their company owned to send them to. It was safer this way, the less people who knew their location, the less likely Jay Turner would be to find them.

Jessica pulled the car to a stop outside the group home, and they both stepped out into the softly falling snow. For a group home, the place looked surprisingly Christmassy. Lights were strung up around the roof, there was a huge blow-up Santa and reindeer in the yard, a wreath with flashing lights hung on the door, and a large Christmas tree was visible in one of the front windows. Spending Christmas there would probably be better than where a lot of the kids had spent previous Christmases, but Adam was still exceedingly glad his little girl would be waking up Christmas morning in her own home with her dad there to give her the best Christmas ever.

At the front door, he pressed the bell and waited. Less than a minute later it was opened by Sawyer. "Kinsley is waiting for you," he announced without preamble. They all wanted this case closed as quickly as possible, so Hayley Hood was safe.

"No troubles?" Jessica asked as they followed the bodyguard down the hall.

"Nothing so far. Hopefully, that man is caught before he does anything more to hurt that little girl. She's a sweet kid, she doesn't deserve any of this." Sawyer had the same anger in his tone that Adam knew was in his own. Sawyer had fourteen-month-old twins, Jackson and Janelle and a four-year-old daughter. Jessica had a five-year-old son.

They all knew what being a parent was all about and seeing someone abuse their own child was just beyond comprehension.

"Hey, Kinsley," he said as they walked into a small room where the little girl was sitting at a table drawing. She stopped what she was doing, looked up at him, gave a small smile then returned to her picture. A middle-aged woman sat in a chair in a corner of the room and stood when they entered.

"I'm the child advocate," she introduced herself. "As long as you keep your questions appropriate, I won't interfere with your interview."

"We will," he assured the woman. They weren't here to traumatize little Kinsley Turner, they just needed to talk to her and see what she could tell them about her sister's death and where her father might be.

"Hi, Kinsley." Jessica took a seat at the table across from the little girl. Although he had a daughter the same age as Kinsley and was comfortable around small children, Jessica usually took over when they had to interview a child because most kids were more comfortable with a strange woman than a strange man.

"Hi," the child said in a small voice.

"What are you drawing?" Jessica asked, taking a crayon and a piece of paper and drawing a picture of her own.

"Me and Leah." Kinsley held up her drawing.

"That's pretty. What are you two doing in your picture?"

"We're baking brownies, we loved to do that, that's why I named the bear Hayley gave me Brownie." Kinsley pointed to the bear that sat in the seat beside her.

"I love to bake too. My son and I will be baking cookies, ginger-bread, and all sorts of goodies on Christmas Eve."

"I like gingerbread," Kinsley said, then returned to her picture.

"What else did you and Leah like to do?"

"She would read to me, or sometimes, when we didn't have any books, she would make up stories."

"That sounds like fun, I love stories."

"She taught me to ride a bike without training wheels. It was her old bike, and it didn't fit her anymore, so she gave it to me."

Jessica smiled. "That was nice of her. It sounds like Leah was a great big sister."

"She was," Kinsley agreed.

"Do you remember the picture you drew of her at school? The one that your teacher talked to you about? Before you came here."

Kinsley nodded.

"In that picture your sister was lying on the ground outside your house. Why did you draw Leah like that?"

Not looking up from her drawing, Kinsley said, "Because Leah fell. She died."

"Do you know where Leah fell from?"

"Uh-huh." The child nodded.

"Where from?"

"From the roof."

"What was Leah doing on the roof?"

"She was running away from daddy."

"How come?"

"Because daddy was hurting her."

"Did he hurt anyone else in your house?"

"He hurt my mommy all the time."

"What about you, did your daddy ever hurt you?" Jessica asked.

"Sometimes, but mostly Leah stopped him."

"How did your daddy hurt Leah the night that she died?"

"He hit her in the face, her nose was bleeding. Leah was scared that he was going to hurt her again, so she climbed out her window. She said she didn't want to let daddy hurt us anymore and that she was going to stop him by telling someone what he was doing."

"Do you know Leah ended up on the ground?"

Kinsley didn't say anything, but she looked worried.

"What's wrong, honey?" Jessica asked.

"Leah told me to hide. There was a space in the back of our closet where you could hide behind the wall. She told me to go there and not come out until she came back with someone to help us."

When the girl paused, Jessica said, "It's okay, sweetheart, you're not in trouble. We just want to know what you saw."

So far Kinsley had been very forthcoming. She wasn't trying to protect her father, she had admitted he abused her sister and her mother. He'd worked cases where cracking abused kids had been harder than getting an abused spouse to turn against their partner. Thankfully Kinsley wasn't one of those kids.

"I heard loud voices, so I crept out."

"Whose voices were they?"

"Daddy and Leah's."

"Did you hear what they were saying?"

"Leah was crying, begging daddy to stop. I went to the window, and I saw Daddy and Leah on the roof. He was holding her here." The child pointed to her wrists. "And her feet weren't on anything."

"What happened next?"

"He put Leah down and told her that she had to go back inside, but Leah said no. So, he pushed her, and she fell."

That was exactly what they had suspected but needed confirmation of. So long as Kinsley passed the examination that would determine whether she understood the difference between the truth and a lie and was deemed competent to testify. Having spent the last ten minutes with the child he knew she would pass. She was a smart little girl, well-spoken, clear in exactly what she had seen and heard. When they arrested Jay Turner, he would stand trial for his older daughter's murder and the testimony of his younger daughter would see him found guilty.

There was only one thing left that they needed to know.

"Kinsley, do you know where your daddy might be right now?" Jessica asked.

"Isn't he at home?"

"No, he's not. We don't know where he is, but we need to find him. Do you know where he might go if he wasn't at home?"

"Uh-uh." Kinsley shook her head.

"Do you have any grandparents, or aunts or uncles, that you go and visit?" Jessica asked. As far as they knew there was no other family, but it was worth asking anyway.

"No. It's just me, and Leah, and Mommy, and Daddy."

"Is there anyone who watched you sometimes if your mommy and daddy couldn't?"

"Sometimes Sarah watched me. She always plays songs for me on her piano, and I dance to them."

They didn't know anything about this Sarah but finding her had just become their number one priority. This visit with Kinsley Turner had gone even better than he had hoped.

~

5:26 P.M.

"All settled in?" Brian asked as Hayley walked down the hall and dropped onto the couch in the safehouse's living room. The apartment was small, with two bedrooms, one bathroom, and one living area. The place was sparsely furnished, but it was comfortable, and more importantly, they would be safe here until Jay Turner was in custody. Only his Uncle Ryan and Brady knew where they were, and as much as he would miss his family if they had to spend the holidays here, he couldn't deny the time alone with Hayley would be nice.

"I guess," Hayley answered his question listlessly. She was a little pale, and she'd been quiet ever since they'd left the offices a little over an hour ago; the stress of the last few days was getting to her.

"What's wrong?" he asked, turning the stove down so the potatoes didn't boil over before joining her on the couch. "I mean, besides the obvious."

"This place." She looked around the room, at the round table with four chairs, the two couches, the coffee table, and the wide-screen TV on the wall. "It doesn't feel like Christmas here. It's only a few days until Christmas, and I might not be able to spend it with my family. We're stuck here. There are no fairy lights, there are no garlands, we don't have a wreath on the door, I don't have my Christmas village. We don't even have a Christmas tree."

He should have known that Hayley needed a Christmas tree. "I'm sorry, Hayley. I'd get you a tree if I could, but we can't leave here, and I don't want anyone coming here just in case Jay Turner is monitoring our friends and follows them."

"It's okay, it's not your fault. I'm glad that I'm safe here, and I'm glad nothing happened to you today. I wouldn't have been able to forgive myself if you'd been hurt when Jay ran us off the road."

"That wouldn't have been your fault," he reminded her. He was glad Jay's abduction attempt had been unsuccessful and he was determined that the man wouldn't get another chance. "Tomorrow, after you've had a good night's sleep, we can see what we can do with what we have to make this place look a little more Christmassy." Once she'd gone to bed he'd have a look around and see if he remembered any good craft ideas from when he used to earn some extra money working at the day camp his church ran over the term breaks.

"I guess," she said non-committedly, shifting on the couch like she was uncomfortable. He'd examined her carefully back at the office. Other than the cut on her forehead she didn't seem to have any other injuries. Even the cut wasn't serious, he'd closed it with butterfly strips and taped a waterproof bandage over the top of it.

"If we have to spend Christmas here, we'll have a great time," he encouraged her, glancing over at the stove. "We'll get a turkey and make more food than either of us can eat. We'll bake pies, and cookies, make eggnog, we'll have a lot of fun."

She mustered up a smile for him. "Yeah, I guess we will. And maybe we can have a second Christmas dinner with our families when we go back home."

"Great idea," he said, heading back to the kitchen to drain and mash the potatoes. "I don't think anyone is going to complain about having two Christmas dinners."

Hayley gave a small laugh. "I don't think anyone would. And maybe we could make this place look a little Christmassy. We could make some paper chains."

"And a handprint wreath for the door," he added.

"Oh, yeah." She laughed again. "What are we going to do for a tree?"

"I'm sure we can figure out something." He ladled some soup into two bowls, scooped some mashed potatoes onto the plates, then added steamed cauliflower and broccoli. Brian set the bowls and plates on two trays, so they could eat on the couch. "What do you want to drink? We have juice, soda, and bottled water."

"What kind of juice?"

"Orange and apple."

"Apple please."

Pouring two glasses of apple juice, he carried the trays over to the coffee table. "Dinner is served."

"This looks amazing," Hayley said, taking her tray and setting it on her lap. "Thanks for cooking again. Tomorrow, I'll cook you dinner."

"Can't wait," he said, flipping on the TV. They watched reruns of Friends while they ate, laughing at the Thanksgiving episode where the gang played touch football in the park, and the Gellers argued over their Geller Cup.

"That was so good," Hayley said, setting her tray back down on the table. She'd eaten about half of the food on her plate, which was better than he'd been hoping. He had expected that given the shock of being run off the road she wouldn't have a very big appetite. *He* didn't have much of an appetite and he wasn't even the one that Jay Turner wanted.

"You look tired. Why don't you sit back here?" He grabbed some pillows, fluffed them up, and then helped prop them up behind Hayley. "Are you cold?" Brian didn't wait for an answer, just grabbed a throw and spread it out over her. "Do you need me to turn the heat up? Do you want some ice cream or I think we have some chocolate? Is the TV too loud? Do you want me to turn it down so you can close your eyes and get some sleep? Or if you want, I can run you a nice hot bubble bath. Or you could take a shower. If you're too tired, I can turn your bed down so you can put on your PJs and go right off to sleep. What?" he asked when he noticed Hayley was looking at him with a bemused smile.

"You're cute when you fuss like this," Hayley told him. "To answer your questions, I'm not cold, so you don't have to turn the heat up. I'm not really hungry so I don't want dessert, but you can have something if you want. The TV is fine. I don't want to close my eyes just yet, I'm not in the mood for a shower or a bath. And I'm not ready for bed. I think that covers everything," she said with a smirk.

"You're not worried about nightmares, are you?" he asked as he gathered up the dishes and went to put the leftovers in the fridge, rinse the dishes, and stack them in the dishwasher.

"No, not really. I don't usually have them, and I didn't have any after the fire, I just feel a weird mix of exhausted and wired."

"The aftereffects of shock. Adrenalin overload and now you're crashing. Why don't we just sit and watch a little TV? Then when you're ready you can go to bed." As much as he wanted to sit down with Hayley and talk about their feelings for each other, he didn't think now was the time to do it. When they did have the conversation, he envisioned some making out afterward, and right now neither of them was in the mood for that.

"Come sit with me." Hayley patted the couch beside her.

Brian sat down next to her, and she immediately spread the blanket over both of them, then snuggled back against the pillows. Their thighs were touching, and the urge to kiss her suddenly overwhelmed him, so maybe making out wasn't completely off his radar.

He had no idea what was playing on the TV, his whole attention was focused on his leg touching her leg. It wasn't really the most romantic of things, and he'd certainly done a whole lot more with other women, but he'd never felt like this about another woman. He had never felt this vice around his heart every time he thought of losing her. He had never felt this fluttering in his stomach over just the thought of something as simple as holding her hand. He had never felt so alone just because they weren't in the same room like a piece of him was missing.

Was this what love felt like?

Hayley shifted, her shoulder resting against his arm, and he very nearly gave up the leave talking about the two of them until another time idea. All he wanted to do was take Hayley into his arms, kiss her until she forgot her own name, then pick her up, carry her to the bedroom, and make love to her until the sun rose.

Her head rested on his shoulder, her breathing deep and even, and he realized that she had drifted off to sleep. Her mind might have felt too wired to sleep, but her exhausted body obviously had other ideas. She was warm and soft against him, and Brian gently maneuvered her so that she was lying down, her head resting on a pillow in his lap.

She was so beautiful.

The light dusting of freckles on her nose and cheeks, the way her dark hair curled slightly around her ears, her long lashes resting against her cheeks, those pink lips that made him imagine what they would feel like pressed to his.

One day.

One day the two of them would explore each other's bodies with their lips and hands.

One day soon he hoped.

For now, he was just going to hold Hayley in his arms and be thankful he was lucky enough to have her in his life. Brian switched off the TV, rested his head back against the couch, and closed his eyes. If he was extra lucky, he might get a little preview of what making out with Hayley would be like in his dreams.

∼

11:32 P.M.

Time flew by so quickly.

Paige Hood looked at the photo in her hands. It had been taken the first Christmas Hayley and Arianna had been with them. The girls were so little, Arianna was just a little baby, and Hayley had been only five years old. She and Elias had adopted the girls in early November, and by Thanksgiving, Hayley had still been too anxious around large groups of people to celebrate the holiday with their extended family, so it had been just the four of them.

By Christmas, Hayley had grown so much more confident in her new family that she had been excited to put up a Christmas tree. She'd never had one before and watching the joy on her face as she saw the tinsel, the fairy lights, and all the decorations had been one of the best moments of her life. They'd left milk and cookies for Santa and carrots for the reindeer, opened gifts together around the tree on Christmas morning, and spent the day with their whole extended family.

Paige had been so proud of her little girl for being so brave.

Now those days felt so far away.

She missed them. Hayley had her own place now, her own life, and while they still saw each other often it wasn't the same. And Arianna was nineteen, in college, and only home for the holidays and the summer. In a couple of years, she would graduate, and then she'd get her own place too.

Twenty years.

It was hard to believe that next year would mark the twentieth anniversary of adopting the girls. It wasn't just Hayley and Arianna that had grown so much in the last two decades, she and Elias had changed a lot too. She was fifty-four now and starting to feel her age. Little twinges in her back that weren't there even a couple of years ago, and she was more tired in the evenings than she had been in her forties. She was glad she had retired from the police force nine years ago, although some days she missed being a cop, she liked working with Ryan and Brady running their business.

As much as she missed having her girls living at home, she was happy that they knew what they wanted to do with their lives, and she was excited for them to fall in love and have families of their own one day soon. She knew Hayley had had a crush on Brian Xander since she was a teenager, and she hoped her daughter would finally get enough courage to tell Brian how she felt. Now that they were twenty-four and thirty, the six-year age gap wasn't an obstacle, and she thought the two of them would make a great couple.

She hoped that they were okay.

If she didn't get to spend Christmas with her daughter, she was glad Hayley was with Brian. And, who knows, maybe this would finally give those two the push they needed to realize that they could find happiness together.

"Come back to bed."

The voice startled her, and she practically jumped out of her skin.

"Sorry," her husband said, appearing beside her. "Didn't mean to scare you."

"It's okay, I guess I was too busy thinking to hear you."

"Reminiscing." Elias reached over and took the photo from her hands. "It feels like just yesterday that we adopted Hayley and Ari."

"It does," she agreed. "Where does the time go?"

"I don't know." Despite her starting to feel her age, her mind didn't feel any different than it had when she had been juggling a demanding job, a husband with a demanding job, and two little girls and their busy schedules. "I miss those days."

"Remember when all we wanted was a full night's sleep," Elias asked with a smile as he wrapped an arm around her shoulders and drew her against him.

"Yeah, now I think I'd trade the no sleep to have the girls back home safe and sound." She hated knowing that her daughter was in trouble and there was nothing she could do to make it better. Paige never felt more impotent than when one of her children was in danger and there was no way for her to fix it. It was nearly ten years since her daughter had been kidnapped as bait to lure her and her partner Ryan into a trap and she still had nightmares about it.

"Hayley will be okay," her husband said, reading her mind.

"I wish she was here with us." Not having her daughter in her sight made her worries so much worse. Jay Turner could have tracked down Hayley and Brian and killed them, and none of them would even know about it.

"There is no one I would trust more with our daughter's safety than Brian Xander," Elias said in such a way that made it clear he was also aware of Hayley's crush.

"You know that she likes Brian, don't you?"

"I've seen that look she gets on her face every time the two of them are in the same room together. It's the same way I used to look at you."

"*Used* to?" She smirked.

"You know I'm going to keep looking at you that way for the rest of our lives." He swept her brown curls out of the way and pressed a kiss to her cheek. "Come back to bed."

"I'm not sleepy. I know Brian will do everything he can to keep Hayley safe, but Jay Turner has been so devious so far. What if he tracks down the safehouse?"

"He won't. Only Ryan and Brady know where they are for that very reason. I know it's hard but try to have faith. Xavier has the entire police department looking for them, and you know he won't stop until Jay Turner is in prison and Hayley is safe."

That was true.

Xavier Montague had been a colleague and friend of hers since he transferred to work out of the same precinct she and Ryan worked out of twenty-five years ago. He had been partners with Ryan's brother Jack, and the four of them had worked several cases together. Even after retiring she had remained close friends with Xavier. His wife Annabelle worked at the center for abused women and children that she and her friends ran together, and she loved Xavier's kids, fourteen-year-old twins JP and Katie, eight-year-old Andy, and seven-year-old Oscar, who they had adopted when he was two.

"I know that Xavier is doing everything he can to keep Hayley safe, and I know Adam and Jessica are working this case as hard as they can, but ..." she trailed off.

"But it's not the same as having her safe and sound and at home with us," her husband finished for her.

"Right." Her gaze drifted back to the photo Elias still held of their first Christmas as a family. "How are we going to celebrate Christmas without Hayley?"

"Because we have to. Because Ari is coming home tomorrow, and the rest of our family and friends want to celebrate with us."

"It won't feel like Christmas without Hayley here with us."

"No, it won't. But if she's not home in time for Christmas, then when this is over, we'll celebrate Christmas again."

It wouldn't be the same though.

Even after Hayley went off to college, they had spent every single Christmas together, and it just wouldn't feel right to be celebrating without her oldest daughter.

"Come to bed now, please?" Elias said.

Christmas wouldn't be the same without Hayley. Still, her husband was right, Arianna was coming all the way home to spend the holidays with them, and her parents and Elias' were getting older. Each holiday they celebrated could be the last they celebrated with them. Plus, there were their siblings, niece, nephews, and friends that she loved every bit as much as her family who would all be excited to spend Christmas together.

Hayley was safe and with the man she loved, she would be okay even if she missed them. Although it might not be Christmas morning when they exchanged gifts the enjoyment of seeing her daughter's face when she opened her presents would still be the same, and they would still stuff themselves full of more food than anyone should eat in one sitting.

It might not be perfect, but the most important thing was that Hayley was safe.

"Okay, we can go back to bed," she agreed.

"Good, it's cold down here." Elias set the photo back on the mantle, took her hand, and led her back upstairs and down the hall to their bedroom.

The doors to Arianna's room and Hayley's old room stood open, and she remembered when she and Elias used to creep down the hall to close them after the girls went to sleep so that they could have a little adult time. Now they didn't have to worry about kids walking in and seeing things they shouldn't.

"I hope you're not too tired." She wriggled her eyebrows at her husband.

"You have something in mind?" He grinned down at her. His hair might be growing gray, and there might be little wrinkles around his eyes, but he was just as handsome as the day they had met.

"Oh, yeah."

"I'm never too tired for that."

Neither was she. She really was pretty lucky, a husband she still adored after almost thirty years of marriage, two gorgeous daughters, a job she loved, and maybe grandkids in the not too distant future.

# CHAPTER
*Four*

December 22nd
10:23 A.M.

Arianna Hood pulled to a stop at a red light, another half an hour or so and she'd be home.

As much as she loved being at college, living in a house with three of her best friends, studying, hanging out, laughing, talking, and having fun in between tests and writing papers, there was nothing like coming home.

Especially at Christmas.

Although it had only been a month since she'd been home to celebrate Thanksgiving with her family, a lot had changed in those few weeks. She had finally found the courage to tell her best friend that she was in love with her brother. She had known Rosie Xander since they were both babies. They'd grown up together, been best friends since they could walk, and she had been in love with Rosie's older brother Zach since she was twelve.

Best friend or potential boyfriend.

That had been the internal debate she had been having with herself for the last seven years.

It would have been easier if it was just a crush, but it wasn't, she loved Zach, and she wanted to spend the rest of her life with him. It also would have been easier if her feelings weren't reciprocated, but they were. Zach felt the same way about her as she felt about him, and they had decided they should talk to his sister and see what she thought about them dating. They had agreed that if Rosie had a problem with it, they wouldn't pursue a relationship. She loved Rosie, and she hadn't wanted to lose her best friend to gain a boyfriend, she had wanted them both.

Having that conversation with her friend was one of the hardest things she had ever had to do. But thankfully, it had worked out perfectly. Rosie had been thrilled and told them they better get married because then the two of them wouldn't just be best friends but sisters too.

So now she was about to celebrate her first holiday with the man she loved as an official couple. She was so excited. As soon as they had talked to Rosie just after Thanksgiving, they had told their families, neither of which seemed particularly surprised at the news, but both of which had been happy for them.

Arianna had to admit she was a little nervous. There was so much pressure on her new relationship. Her mom had known Zach's dad since before they were born, they'd even dated briefly before her mom met her dad, and then a few years later Zach's dad reconnected with his childhood sweetheart. She really loved Zach, and she wanted the two of them to still be together and in love like their parents when they were their age.

As nervous as she was, she was equally as excited. This year they wouldn't have to just sneak looks at one another, wondering if the other felt the same way they did. This Christmas they would be able to hold hands, kiss under the mistletoe, and be like a real couple.

The light changed to green, and she drove off. Arianna turned up the volume, and for the next twenty minutes she sang along—woefully out of tune, but what she lacked in talent she made up for in vigor—to an array of Christmas carols and songs. By the time she pulled into her parents' street, she was brimming with Christmassy glee. She couldn't wait to get inside, hug her parents and sister, set her gifts under the tree, have lunch, and catch up on everything that had happened over the last few weeks. Then she was having dinner with Zach, who had driven back from college yesterday.

Pulling to a stop outside her parents' house, she was filled with nostalgia when she saw the big blow-up Christmas tree surrounded by a family of lighted reindeer in the front yard. She still remembered the year they'd gotten it; she'd been six and Hayley had been eleven. They'd spent ages in the store deciding which of the large blow-up displays to buy. Every Christmas since, they'd set it up in the yard. For many years after they'd bought it, Arianna would sit at her bedroom window at night and stare out at the glowing scene.

Home really was something special, but this house wouldn't be her home for much longer. It would always be the first real home she'd had, and it would always be a place she could come to when she needed love and support, but soon she would be making a home of her own with Zach.

They'd talked about it. She was only nineteen, and he was only twenty, both of them hoped to follow in their parents' footsteps—her mother and Zach's father—and join the police force. It was going to be a busy but stressful time of their lives, and they thought they would face it better together than on their own. So, the summer after they graduated —only two and a half years away—they were going to be married. She'd be twenty-one by then, and Zach would be twenty-two. They'd be young but they'd both been set wonderful examples of how a successful relationship worked by their parents and extended family, so she knew they would be okay.

It was snowing out, so she turned off the engine and shrugged into her coat, wrapped her scarf around her neck a couple of times, pulled a beanie down low so it covered her ears and most of her forehead, then grabbed her suitcase from the front seat and stepped out into the cold.

In her peripheral vision, she saw someone walking down the sidewalk but didn't pay them much attention. She wanted to get inside and start celebrating Christmas.

She was just locking the car when she noticed a shadow looming over her.

Arianna turned around expecting to see someone who needed help, or maybe one of her family or friends.

Instead, it was a man with brown hair and blue eyes.

She'd never seen him before.

"You're not Hayley," he growled when he got a look at her face.

Her sister?

Why did he think she was Hayley?

What did he want?

"No, I'm her little sister, Arianna," she said. The man must be a friend of Hayley's or maybe he worked with her. Her sister was very dedicated to her job.

"Sister, huh?" He looked thoughtful, and again she wondered who he was and what he was doing here.

"I can pass on a message to her if you like," she offered.

"Oh, you're going to pass on a message all right." He smiled, but it wasn't a nice smile.

Alarm bells went off in her head.

Something was wrong.

Whoever this man was he wasn't here just to see her sister about something innocent like work.

"Excuse me," she said, trying to walk around him so she could get up the path and to the front door.

"I don't think so." The man grabbed her arm as she tried to pass him.

"Let go of me." She yanked her arm but couldn't break it free of his iron grip.

"I bet Hayley would do anything to get her little sister back," the man said, although it seemed more to himself than to her, and he began to drag her toward a van parked across the street.

This wasn't happening.

This man wasn't going to kidnap her.

Especially not to use in some plot to hurt her sister.

The man was much bigger than her, and despite her best efforts to stop him, he was already dragging her further away from her car and her parents' house. If he got her into his van, she would never come home alive. She was the daughter of a cop and wanted to be one when she graduated. She knew plenty of statistics, just like she knew that her best chance of getting out of this was to scream at the top of her lungs.

Arianna opened her mouth and screamed.

And screamed.

And screamed.

The sound startled the man trying to abduct her and he momentarily loosened his grip on her.

That was all the advantage she needed.

She yanked as hard as she could and flew backward, falling down and landing on her bottom on the road.

The man leaned down to reclaim his grip on her, but she was still screaming, and the street was starting to fill with people.

"Ari?"

She snapped her head sideways at the sound of her mother's voice and saw both her parents come running out the front door.

Knowing he was beaten, the man ran to the van, jumped in, and tore off down the street.

"Honey? Are you hurt?" Mom asked as she and Dad materialized beside her.

"I'm all right," she murmured, still struggling to believe what had almost happened.

"Who was that?" her father demanded.

"A man, he thought I was Hayley."

"Jay Turner," her mom muttered like this all made sense.

Only to her none of this made any sense at all.

She didn't know who Jay Turner was, she didn't know how he knew her sister or what he wanted with her, and she had no idea why she had very nearly been abducted.

All she knew was that her heart was racing, her pulse pounding, her palms sweating, and her eyes were growing watery. She let her parents wrap their arms around her and lead her inside, but even the warmth of the house and her parents' embrace couldn't erase the icy ball of fear that had taken up residence in her stomach. Arianna wasn't sure anything ever could.

~

12:13 P.M.

"I am so grateful that your uncle had a sewing machine left here for me," Hayley said. She loved the sound of the whirring needle, and sewing had worked wonders on her frazzled nerves to be able to spend the morning finishing off the last of her Christmas gifts. Even if she wouldn't be able to spend Christmas Day with her family, she still wanted to know that all the gifts were finished.

"Uncle Ryan knows you well," Brian said. She'd been tired and distracted last night and hadn't realized until they got up this morning that Ryan and Brady had brought the box with her Christmas gifts and her sewing machine here before she and Brian arrived.

She had spotted them as soon as she came through to the living room at six this morning, and ever since, she had been practically glued to her machine. Brian had coaxed her away to eat a little breakfast and she suspected he would soon be trying to do it again for lunch.

But she wasn't hungry.

It wasn't that she was nauseous, sick, or anything else she was just enjoying this. It kept her distracted, so she didn't have to think about Jay Turner, and she knew that as soon as she stopped all of those fears and anxieties were going to come rushing back.

"He does," she agreed, beyond grateful for what Ryan and Brady had done for her. They ran a private security firm, they had both been cops, and their natural instinct was to focus on her safety, that was their priority. Yet they had gone out of their way to make sure she was comfortable and as happy as she could be while stuck here.

"You're really good," Brian said, watching her with a little bit of awe on his face. He had been watching her all morning. Maybe it should have made her a little uncomfortable, but it didn't, she just loved being with him too much.

"Thanks."

"I can't believe you've made one of those for everyone in our family in just twelve months."

"It was a lot of work." There were her parents, her sister, two sets of grandparents, her aunt and her family, her two uncles and their families, and that was just the relatives.

Then there was Brian's family, his parents, two sisters, their husbands, and Elise's baby daughter. There was Sophie and her little brother and parents, and Brian's Uncle Jack and his wife and three kids, including their eight-year-old daughter Dotty who had Downs Syndrome, and the two foster kids they had living with them at the moment as well as Xavier and Annabelle Montague and their four kids.

She'd made some for Brady, his wife Aurora, their kids, and her friends Sawyer, his family, and Samara. All in all, that made a total of fifty-four Christmas books she'd had to make this year, which evened out to four and a half a month, or a little over one a week. She had been rushed off her feet trying to find every spare second she could to work on them, but she had loved every moment of it. It was her way of expressing her love for the people in her life that were special to her.

"You're totally amazing, you know that right?" Brian stood and came to join her at the table.

"It's nothing." Hayley brushed off his praise.

"It's not nothing. These are absolutely gorgeous, you put so much work into them."

"Once I got the pattern going it wasn't so hard. Most of them are pretty similar, except for Dotty's, she always gets one a little bit special." She adored Jack and Laura Xander's youngest daughter. The little girl was just the sweetest thing, and neither she nor anyone in her family ever let her Down's Syndrome hold her back.

"Dotty deserves it, she's such a gem. My mom used to sew when we were younger. I don't think she did much once we all got older though. Although with a grandchild now and a second one on the way, I think she'll probably start up again. I always thought being able to take bits of material and turn them into something was pretty cool. Maybe you could teach me."

"*You* want to learn to sew?" she asked with a laugh.

"Hey, don't laugh." Brian pouted, but his blue eyes twinkled. "I'm never going to be as good as you, but it would be fun to be able to sew teddy bears and things for my little niece and soon-to-be niece or nephew."

"Okay, I can teach you. All I have to do is finish up Dotty's Christmas book, and then we can try making something with the left-over material. It's the perfect time to teach you since we're going to have a ton of extra time on our hands, and we can't leave this apartment."

"Perfect." Brian smiled at her, and the look on his face said he was going to say more, but the burner phone that Brady and Ryan had left here in case they needed to contact them in an emergency began to ring.

Their eyes met, anxiety passing between them.

What had happened?

If Jay Turner was in police custody, someone would have driven here to tell them in person.

Since they were calling instead that implied it was bad news.

Had Jay made a move to try to get his daughter back?

Had Kinsley been hurt? Or worse kidnapped?

Sawyer was watching over the little girl. Had he been hurt?

Hayley prayed that everyone was okay.

Brian picked up the phone but crossed to the far side of the room before answering. Her sewing forgotten, Hayley watched his face as he spoke to whoever was on the other end, trying to decipher what was going on by his expression and the look in his eyes. But he was like a statue, betraying nothing of whatever was going on, and so she was forced to sit there, wringing her hands in her lap, and waiting until he hung up.

"Who was it?" she demanded the second Brian set the phone down.

"It was Ryan."

"What did he want?" Hayley had to force herself not to hold her breath as she waited for his answer.

He hesitated, and that amped up her anxiety.

"Brian, what did Ryan want? I know it wasn't good news. Is it Kinsley? Sawyer? Maria?" Maybe Jay Turner had taken another go at his wife and ended up killing her this time.

"No, it's not Kinsley, Sawyer, or Maria."

"Then what?" Had there been an accident maybe? Something unrelated to this case? Arianna had been going to drive back from college today to spend Christmas with their family. Had her sister crashed her car or something?

Brian reached out and took her hands, gently prying them out of the death grip she had them twisted up in. He held onto them, his thumbs brushing absently across her knuckles. "It's Arianna."

"What happened?" she asked tightly. She didn't know what she would do if anything had happened to her little sister. They might not be biologically related, but they had been sisters Ari's entire life, and she loved Arianna so much.

"Jay Turner must have figured out where your parents live, he was waiting outside their house. When Arianna pulled up, he thought she was you and tried to grab her. She told him who she was, but he decided to try to take her anyway. Maybe just to hurt her or maybe to try to force your hand and get you to give yourself over to him."

Hayley just stared at him.

It was like he was speaking gibberish.

She wasn't sure how long she sat there, staring blankly at Brian.

Maybe seconds, maybe minutes, maybe hours for all she knew.

Then she snapped and the next thing she realized she was jumping to her feet and running toward the door.

Brian jumped up after her and caught her before she got outside, wrapping an arm around her, yanking her backward, and holding her tight against his body. "Where do you think you're going?"

"To Ari," she said, struggling in his grip. She had to see her sister, she had to know that Arianna was okay.

"Your sister is fine. She screamed, spooked Jay, and he ran off. She's not hurt, just shaken up. She's with your mom and dad."

Hayley didn't care.

She needed to see that with her own eyes to believe it.

"Let me go." She squirmed, but Brian just tightened his hold on her.

"No. Don't you see that's exactly what he wants? He wants you to be so scared of what he's going to do, or who he's going to threaten to go after that you either just go to him, or you get complacent with your safety, and he can get to you. You're safe here, and I'm sure your mom will make sure that Ari is safe too. This is where you need to be right now, and I'm not going to let you leave."

With that, the wind was taken out of her sails.

Hayley still wanted desperately to go and see her sister, but the last time she hadn't listened to Brian and assumed that everything would be okay their car had been run off the road. She wouldn't do anything to endanger Brian's safety again. Besides, she suspected that Brian would handcuff her to the table if he had to to prevent her from leaving this apartment.

Tears came next.

In an uncontrollable flood.

Without loosening his hold, Brian turned her around, and Hayley buried her face in his chest and sobbed.

Why was this happening?

Why couldn't Jay just accept that it was over? They knew he had killed Leah, he wasn't getting Kinsley back, and he was going to prison. Killing her wasn't going to change any of that.

Curling her fingers into Brian's sweater, Hayley clung to him. She just wanted this to be over.

~

1:47 P.M.

"Well, we spoke to everyone on the street, and no one got a license plate," Jessica Spears said dejectedly as she and her partner stood outside the Hood house where a couple of hours ago Arianna Hood had very nearly been abducted.

"And we still haven't managed to find out who this Sarah is that Kinsley Turner told us watched her sometimes," Adam said.

They had spent the previous day from their visit with Kinsley until they went home to their children trying to find out who the woman was so they could interview her. So far, they hadn't had any luck.

Jessica was worried about the woman. Jay was spinning out of control. He was so obsessed with getting revenge on Hayley for removing his daughter from his home that he couldn't think of anything else. She wouldn't put it past the man to be using Sarah's house as his place to hide out and had at worst already killed the woman, and at best, had just tied her up and kept her prisoner in her home.

They really needed to find out who Sarah was and where she lived.

"He's fixated on Hayley for now, but we were there that day too. He could change his focus any time and decide to come after either of us," Adam said.

She'd thought of that.

And it wasn't a pleasant thought.

"Or he could go after Freddie or Claire," she voiced the worry that had been at the back of her mind ever since they'd taken Kinsley.

"I think we should ask for patrol cars to make regular runs down our streets. When he thinks he's in danger of being caught he seems backs off, hopefully having increased patrols will deter him from trying to go after either of the kids."

"Hopefully," she echoed. She didn't know what she would do if anything ever happened to Freddie. He was her world, her heart, the love she felt for her son she couldn't even put into words. "We better go in and talk to Arianna. Maybe she knows something that will help."

"Yeah, hopefully," Adam said, but it was clear he wasn't going to be holding his breath.

She wasn't much more optimistic than her partner was.

So far this case wasn't moving forward. Jay kept upping the ante and making bolder attempts to get what he wanted, but they weren't having any luck finding where he had squirreled himself away.

They walked up to the front door, which was immediately thrown open by a frazzled-looking Paige. Jessica could empathize. If it was her daughter being stalked by a violent man, and then her other daughter almost abducted by that same man, she would be out of her mind with worry.

"Did anyone see anything useful?" Paige Hood demanded.

"No. A few neighbors came running outside when they heard Arianna screaming, they saw a man pulling her toward a van, but no one got a license plate. A few people thought they got a partial plate, but none of the numbers matched up, they all saw something different," Jessica explained.

"You'll run them though, in all the combinations?"

"We will," she assured the older woman.

"Where's Arianna?" Adam asked.

"In the living room," Paige replied, then abruptly turned and headed toward the living room.

She and Adam closed the door and then followed. In the living room they found Arianna sitting on the couch, a steaming mug of hot chocolate clutched so tightly in her hands that her knuckles were white. Elias Hood sat on one side of his daughter, and Paige had taken a seat on the other. Both of them were sitting so close to Ari that they were practically on top of her.

Brady Crowley and Ryan Xander were also here, and she wondered if anyone had called Brian and Hayley to tell them what had happened. Although Jessica didn't know where the two were hiding, she assumed they had an untraceable burner phone, so even if Jay Turner could hack their phones he wouldn't be able to find Hayley by tracing their calls.

"You want something to drink?" Brady asked.

"Anything hot," Jessica said, rubbing her hands together as she took a seat on the other couch. Spending the morning outside, standing on people's front porches as they interviewed the neighbors had chilled her to the bone.

"I'll go make some coffee," Brady said, heading for the kitchen.

"How has he been able to do all of this? And stay off the radar for days?" Paige asked, frustrated.

"From what we know of him this seems out of character. He hasn't ever held a job for more than a couple of months. He spends most of his time drinking and beating his wife and kids, and he dropped out of school when he was fifteen. And yet he found somewhere to hide out after setting Hayley's house on fire, and was able to contact his wife and get her to come to him. He was able to find out where Kinsley was and knew that eventually Hayley would show up there. He was able to find out where she lived and make an attempt to grab her. And he's found a place to hide out where we haven't been able to find him even though the entire police force is looking for him. We have obviously been underestimating him all along," Ryan said.

"We aren't underestimating him anymore," Jessica assured him. "When we spoke to Kinsley, she mentioned a woman named Sarah who sometimes looked after her. We're trying to track down that woman. We think there's a possibility that he might be hiding out at her house."

"What if you can't find this Sarah woman?" Paige asked. "He's proven he's determined to kill Hayley and that he won't stop until he succeeds. She can't stay in hiding forever."

"We'll find him," Jessica promised. "Yes, so far it looks like we've underestimated him, but he's so angry it's clouding his thinking, and sooner rather than later he's going to slip up, and we'll get him."

"We're hoping Arianna might be able to help us," Adam said.

"It happened so quickly, I don't think I can tell you anything helpful," Arianna immediately told them.

She didn't want Arianna to block any memories she might have by talking herself out of it. "Why don't we just go through what happened and see what you do remember. No pressure. I know everything probably happened so fast that it all became kind of a blur, but anything at all that you remember could be helpful. So why don't you just tell us from the beginning what happened?"

Arianna sighed like she had already gone through the attempted abduction several times. "I was driving home for the holidays. I parked in the street. It was snowing so I put on my coat, scarf, beanie, then grabbed my bag and got out of the car."

So, it was likely that Jay had thought it was Hayley getting out of the car. Both Hayley and Ari had the same long dark hair and were approximately the same height. From a distance it would have been hard to tell them apart.

"How far toward the house had you gotten before he approached you?" Adam asked.

"I didn't move at all. I was just locking the car when I noticed him."

"What did he say?"

"He was surprised that I wasn't Hayley, and then when I said that I was her sister he looked thoughtful, like even though it wasn't what he was expecting that was good news. I thought he was a friend or colleague and said I'd pass along a message. I didn't know that anything was going on with my sister." Arianna paused to shoot both her parents an irritated frown.

"We were going to tell you when you got home," Elias told his daughter.

"We didn't want you to worry," Paige added.

"He said something to the effect of that's right I'd pass on a message," Arianna continued. "When I tried to walk around him, he grabbed my arm and said he bet Hayley would do anything to get me back. He was big, and I knew that he was too strong for me to fight off, so I screamed. That's what my mom always taught me, if I was ever in danger, just scream, it would startle the attacker and alert people in the area that something is going on. It worked, he loosened his grip, and I was able to get free, then when he heard people coming he ran off."

"Did you get his license plate?" Adam asked.

"No, I'm sorry." Arianna dropped her gaze to her lap.

"Is there anything else that you remember?" Jessica asked. "Something about what he was wearing, the sound of his voice, or the way he smelled?"

"No—oh," she paused, looking thoughtful now. "He did smell odd."

Jessica couldn't count the number of times that something a victim had smelled ended up helping them find the perpetrator. "Odd how?"

"Not how I'd expect a man his age to smell."

"What did he smell like?" Adam asked.

"Lavender and camphor, he smelled like my grandmother."

Lavender and camphor, grandmother smells. Could this be more proof that Jay Turner was hiding out at Sarah's house?

2:02 P.M.

It was like fitting all the pieces of a puzzle together.

Now Jay was almost pleased that he didn't have Hayley Hood in his clutches just yet.

Not that he wasn't going to crush her when he got his hands on her. Because he was.

But he got a certain amount of pleasure from knowing that she must be out of her mind with fear knowing that he was coming for her.

He hoped she knew he'd very nearly succeeded in abducting her sister. When he'd managed to track down her parents' address—which had been surprisingly easy thanks to a drinking buddy who owed him who worked at the DMV—he had assumed that was where she was hiding out since he set her house on fire.

His hours of sitting and waiting had paid off. When a car had come driving down the street and pulled to a stop outside the Hood house, he had been positive it was Hayley. Then a young woman with long dark hair had gotten out of the car, wearing a scarf and beanie, he hadn't been able to see her face, but he hadn't thought he needed to. He'd been so sure that it was Hayley.

Despite his initial shock when the woman turned around, and he realized that she was much too young to be the social worker he wanted, he quickly realized that it didn't really matter. As soon as the teenager identified herself as Hayley's sister—which seemed like a stupid thing to do, he was a stranger, and yet she had readily told him who she was without finding out anything about him first—he knew that this was a golden opportunity to get to Hayley.

If he took her sister, he was sure she would have done whatever he said to get him to let the girl go unharmed.

Not that he ever would have let her go *completely* unharmed.

The sister was a pretty girl, and since it was too risky for him to contact his wife again so soon after last time, he certainly had some built-up needs that she could have attended to.

But he would have let the kid go to get Hayley, she was what he wanted, not the sister. It really was a shame that it hadn't worked out.

Jay tossed his head back and downed the rest of his can of beer in one long swig, then dropped the can on the floor beside him.

He was restless.

He wanted to be out, working on tracking down Hayley, but it was getting riskier.

And he was running out of places to look.

Since he had set her house on fire, he knew she wouldn't be going back there. Since he had tried to run her and the man off the road on their way back from the group home where his kid was, he knew she wouldn't be going back there. Since he had nearly abducted her sister at their parents' house, she wouldn't be going back there either.

But she was somewhere.

Just because he didn't know where to look next, it didn't mean he wouldn't figure it out. He had to. Anything else was unacceptable.

Last night he had dreamed about what he would do when he had Hayley. He had beaten, stabbed, drowned, shot, strangled, and set her on fire. It had been a disappointment to wake up after all of that.

Not a complete disappointment.

He wasn't alone here which was definitely a good thing.

For him at least, he thought with a snicker. Not so good for his roommate though. He was pretty sure that right about now she was wishing she was anywhere but here.

Standing, he stretched, enjoying the cracking feeling in his spine. He crunched his knuckles next, they were a little sore from the lesson he had given Maria the other night. When he finally got his hands on Hayley and ended her life, he was going to have to decide what his next move was. There was no way he was walking away without his wife and his kid. He just hadn't figured out yet how he was going to get them.

He was getting sick of thinking.

As entertaining as it had been working this puzzle to find the solutions, he was tired of that now.

He deserved a little break.

Some relaxation time.

Grabbing another beer, he left the kitchen where he had spent the last couple of hours and headed down the hall. He swayed a little as he went, that familiar alcohol buzz flowed through his veins. It was the way he had lived his life since he was twelve and had his very first beer. At twelve, he had snuck one of his dad's cans once the old man was so drunk he could no longer comprehend his surroundings. When he was big enough that his father no longer tried to beat him up, he didn't bother to hide the fact that he drank his dad's beer. Instead of sneaking one up to his room and drinking in the early hours of the morning as he looked out at the dark sky and the moon, he would just take one when he felt like it and would even down it in front of his father.

Alcohol wasn't just a drink to him.

It was a way of life.

It was *his* way of life.

Using the wall to steady himself, Jay swung open the door to the master bedroom, his gaze going immediately to the walk-in wardrobe on the other side of the room. He'd barricaded it by shoving a crowbar between the two door handles, but he could see that his roommate had tried to get out.

Strolling across the carpet, he pressed his ear to the closet door. Inside he could hear soft whimpers. She knew he was here. That turned him on. He liked knowing that she was afraid of him, he liked knowing that his wife was afraid of him, and that his daughters were too.

It was a thrill unlike any other.

Never again was he going to allow another person to control him like his father had tried to. Every time he struck Maria, it was like erasing every strike his father had ever given him.

Taking hold of the crowbar, he pulled it out slowly, each second that ticked by the thrill was growing. He was completely and utterly in control here, and she knew it.

The first thing that hit him was the smell.

A putrid mix of urine, feces, vomit, and fear.

Inside the closet was dark, but he could make out a shape huddled deep in the back corner partially obscured by evening dresses on hangers and a pile of shoes.

"Come out," he ordered. She couldn't really think that he wouldn't see her there. There was nowhere she could hide. This may technically be her house, but while he was here it was his.

She didn't move.

That was not a smart move.

He was already angry with Leah, with Kinsley, with Maria, with Hayley Hood, he didn't need anything else to add to that or it was very likely he would explode.

"I said, come out," he repeated. He tried to over-enunciate each word, but his alcohol-addled brain slurred the words, which was probably more menacing. She knew what he was going to do to her if she didn't obey, so why was she making things worse for herself?

Still the woman stayed where she was, but he heard her whimper.

Stalking over to her, he reached down and grabbed the first body part his hand connected with. Pulling her out by the elbow, he shook her as hard as he could, her head snapped backward and forward, and she groaned again.

Unfortunately for her, that sound only turned him on more.

"You should have listened," he told her as he dragged her out of the closet and threw her down on the floor.

Terrified eyes stared up at him, but he didn't meet their gaze for more than a second before it settled on her cheek. The bruise he'd given her earlier when he'd broken down her door, overpowered her, and thrown her in the closet had grown darker. The mottled mix of blacks and blues filled him with memories, some old, some new, but it also filled him with anger.

He wanted more black and blue.

He wanted to see more bruises on her.

The woman hadn't really done anything wrong, but Maria wasn't here, and neither was Hayley Hood, so as the closest and most convenient target she was going to take the brunt of his rage.

And he had a lot of rage.

Jay delivered a swift kick to her ribs, then crouched down. "You should have come out when I told you to," he whispered.

5:39 P.M.

"Do you want to watch TV?" Brian asked.

"No, thank you." Hayley shook her head.

"Do you want to wrap Christmas gifts?"

"No, thank you."

"Do you want to bake gingerbread or something? The kitchen is fully stocked."

"No, thank you."

"Do you want to play a board game?"

"No, thank you."

"Do you want to rent a spaceship and fly to Mars?"

"No, thank you."

"Hayley," he said, exasperated. Ever since she'd found out that Jay Turner had tried to kidnap her sister, she had been walking around in a daze. Other than her initial meltdown she hadn't cried again, just flitted around the house if he asked her to help with dinner, set the table, or anything else or sat stiffly in a corner of the couch and stared into space. He wanted to snap her out of it, but he didn't know how.

"What?" She turned her head slowly to look at him.

"You're not listening to a word I've been saying."

"I was," she protested.

"Okay then what was the last thing I suggested we do to hang out tonight?"

"Umm ..." She looked at him helplessly. "Okay, maybe I was a little distracted."

"A little?" he teased, jabbing her in the ribs.

"Okay, more than a little," she acknowledged with a small smile. "I don't care what we do tonight, whatever you want is fine with me."

"What about a game?" His family had been big on board games when he was growing up. They'd had a family fun night at least once a month, even when he was a teenager, and although at the time he would never have admitted it out loud, he had actually enjoyed those nights. Sitting around the kitchen table, laughing, talking, eating snacks, bickering good-naturedly, the competitive levels of those nights were off the charts, put four siblings together and they couldn't be anything but.

"Sure," Hayley agreed without a lot of enthusiasm. That was okay he knew just what game to play to finally get a spark out of her.

"Be right back," he told her as he headed down the hall to his room. When Uncle Ryan and Brady were organizing this place for them to stay in there were a couple of things he'd asked them to pack for him. The sewing machine and the gifts Hayley had been making was one, his Christmas gift for her in case they ended up spending the holidays here was another, and this particular board game was the third.

When he returned to the living room, he saw that Hayley had sunk back into her daze. Her back ramrod straight, her hands clasped tightly in her lap—so tightly he could see her knuckles were white—her gaze blank as she stared at the TV without seeing what was on it.

"Time to play," he said, forcing some cheer into his voice to push away the worry. He didn't know how Hayley was going to get through this. So far Jay had continued to slip through the cops' fingers, and he had to proceed under the assumption that that could continue to happen for days or weeks, possibly even months. As her bodyguard—and her friend—it wasn't just his job to keep her alive and in one piece, it was also his job to make sure she made it through this intact psychologically as well. Or at least come out of it as okay as she could be after living through someone's attempts to kill her.

Brian had expected to repeat himself several times before Hayley realized he was in the room, but she immediately looked over, her eyes falling to the box he held in his hands.

"Is that what I think it is?" she asked, shocked.

"Sure is," he said, joining her on the couch and setting the game on the coffee table.

"I can't believe you still have it." Hayley was still staring at the box like she couldn't believe it existed.

"Of course I do. I wouldn't throw this away."

A little color brightened Hayley's cheeks. "I spent so long choosing that. I second-guessed myself so many times. I thought you probably would have thrown it away the next day, not kept it for ten years."

"This was the sweetest, most thoughtful gift I've ever been given," he told her, and he wasn't lying. Hayley had given him this game of Operation as a Christmas gift when she was fourteen, and he was twenty. Their families always did a Secret Santa and that year she had gotten him, the limit was ten dollars because the idea was to be creative and thoughtful, not spend a lot of money.

"You were pre-med. At the time you wanted to be a surgeon like your dad, and I knew how much you loved board games, so I thought you might have liked it. But I was so nervous about giving it to you, I didn't want to look childish or stupid, and I didn't want to give away that ..." Hayley trailed off, but he knew what she had been going to say.

"It was a great gift, Hales. This was my favorite game as a kid, I would spend hours playing it."

"Then let's play," she said brightly, a little *too* brightly, like she was trying to hide something.

He didn't push her on it, and they put all the little white plastic Funatomy pieces into their spots. They shuffled the two sets of cards and dealt out the Specialist ones, setting the Doctor cards beside the Operation board. "You want to go first?"

"Sure." Hayley picked up a Doctor card. "I got the butterflies in Cavity Sam's stomach," she announced. Picking up the tweezers, she positioned them carefully over the butterfly piece and slowly lowered them down into the small hole. She clamped them together, clutching the plastic butterfly between them, then began to bring them up. She almost had it out when she bumped the side, and Cavity Sam buzzed, his nose lighting up. "I didn't get it."

"I have the Specialist card for the butterflies," Brian said, taking the tweezers. In one smooth movement, he pinched them together, lowered them into the hole, picked up the butterfly and pulled it out. "Got it." He grinned.

"I was never any good at this game," Hayley said. "My hands aren't steady enough."

"Here I'll help you," he said. "Take another card."

"It's supposed to be your turn."

Brian grinned. "I think we can bend the rules a little. Here you go." He picked up another card. "It's the charley horse. Come sit here." He patted the edge of the couch in front of him. Hayley gave him a funny look but complied. "Take the tweezers." Once she did, he put his hand over hers. "You want to move confidently. Don't second-guess yourself. Just one smooth motion, down, grasp the horse, then back up again." Guiding her hand with his, he did exactly what he'd just said. The piece came out without setting off the buzzer. "We got it."

"Yeah, we did," she agreed, her breath hitching.

"See, just nice and smooth." His own breath hitched as her hair tickled his nose. Her body was right up against his, her back to his chest, her slender neck right by his mouth and it was all he could do not to trail a line of kisses along it.

"What made you change your mind about going into surgery," Hayley asked. "You would have been so good at it."

"I guess the cop genes in me were too strong. I didn't just want to be a cop though, and since I was already pre-med, when my uncle and your mom took over the private security firm it seemed like the perfect compromise. I still got to practice medicine, but I also got to help keep people safe."

"You do so much more than just keep people safe. You volunteer at the women and children's center our families run and at a free clinic."

He shrugged even though she couldn't see him. "Uncle Ryan and your mom pay me well so that I can be available whenever they need me, but that's not too often, and I don't just want to sit around and do nothing. Volunteering keeps me busy and I enjoy it, and I've gotten used to having to drop everything to go to work when they need me."

"Like with me. With this," Hayley said quietly.

"No, not like this," he rebuked gently. "You know this is different. That *you're* different."

"Right. Because we're friends."

"But we're not just friends are we. You like me, you've had a crush on me since you were a little girl."

"I ... uh ... I ... umm ... not a ... well you see ... it's really more of a ..." she trailed off helplessly, and he couldn't help but chuckle.

"It's okay, Hayley. I always knew that you liked me, but back then you were just a kid. Now you're a smart, strong, courageous, beautiful woman."

"W-what?" she spluttered.

"The last few days, spending all this time together, I know we're not just friends, and I'm not just physically attracted to you." Gently he brushed her hair over her shoulders and pulled it to the side, exposing more of her neck. Brian traced his fingertips along her soft, white skin and felt her shiver beneath his touch. Leaning down he whispered his lips across her neck. "I'm falling for you, Hayley."

∼

6:04 P.M.

. . .

Falling for you.

What exactly did that mean?

Did it mean that he just kind of liked her? Did it mean that he was just feeling sorry for her? Did it mean that he realized that she was hopelessly in love with him and he reciprocated her feelings?

Hayley had no idea.

Abruptly, she jerked off the couch and walked to the wall. "What do you mean you always knew that I liked you?" Before waiting for an answer, she began to stalk up and down the room like a caged animal. "I don't understand. What does that mean? How could you know? I never said anything. The only people that know are Sophie and my mom, and I know neither of them would say anything. So how could you know? And *always*, what exactly does that mean? How long have you known? I don't understand. I don't—"

"Hayley, stop." Brian appeared beside her, took hold of her shoulders, and physically prevented her from continuing pacing.

"No," she said, trying to dislodge herself from his grip. This was too much right now. She couldn't even deal with what was going on with Jay Turner and her sister and knowing someone wanted to kill her. There was no way she could also deal with trying to figure out what Brian meant and what he felt and whether he was trying to tell her that he wanted them to be a couple because he reciprocated her feelings.

"I knew I shouldn't have said anything right now." Brian looked upset. "The timing is all wrong. I was going to wait until this thing with Jay Turner was sorted out, but the more I'm around you ..." he trailed off.

"What?" she asked. She needed to hear him say it.

"I know you've had a crush on me since you were a kid—"

"Nine," she inserted.

"Since you were nine," he amended with a small smile.

"If you knew then why didn't you say anything?"

"Why didn't *you* say anything?" he shot back.

Stumped, she had nothing to say to that.

She didn't know why she'd never confessed her feelings to Brian.

At first, it was because she was too young and he was so much older, but then once they'd both gotten older, she still hadn't been able to bring herself to tell him.

Sensing that she didn't have an answer, Brian continued, "When Paige and Elias first adopted you, you were just this little kid, you were like another little cousin. When you were fifteen and I was twenty-one, it was too big an age gap. I was an adult and I still saw you as a kid. You were a friend, I loved spending time with you, but back then the six years was too big a gap, and while I knew you liked me, I didn't reciprocate those feelings."

Although she knew he wasn't finished speaking, she couldn't help but tense at his words.

She'd known that.

At fifteen a relationship with a twenty-one-year-old pre-med college student wouldn't have been appropriate, but it still hurt to know that he hadn't felt the same way about her as she had about him.

"The other day when I heard that you had been attacked on the job everything changed. I realized that you weren't a kid anymore, you were a woman, a beautiful woman. I knew that I liked you, I knew that I was attracted to you, but I thought that was it. But watching you these last few days, how you've dealt with everything, I'm not just attracted to you. I'm falling for you. Fast."

Hayley just stared.

For so long she had wanted to hear him say those words, but now that he had said them it felt surreal.

She didn't want to believe it because she was afraid of getting her hopes up too high and then having them dashed.

She didn't think that Brian really understood the depth of her feelings. She hadn't ever really dated because she had been in love with Brian since her teens. But it wasn't that way for him, he'd dated a lot over the years, and she knew a lot of those relationships had been serious. His feelings for her were new and no doubt fueled by the drama and high stakes of the last few days.

If they weren't in the same place, then she didn't want to date Brian because if it didn't work out, she could lose someone she had loved since she was a kid.

"Brian," she started. She had to explain to him just how much she loved him.

"You don't have to," he said.

"Don't have to what?" she asked, confused.

"I get it. I know what you feel." He lifted a hand and placed it on her chest, right over her heart. Butterflies immediately made themselves known in her stomach. "You love me. I'm sorry I didn't realize that sooner. But I know it now, and you don't have to worry that I don't understand or that what I feel isn't real. It's real." He gave a chuckle. "It's way real. Here." One of his hands was still over her heart, and with his other, he picked up one of her hands and pressed it to his chest. "Feel it. Feel what's in my heart."

Her hand warmed.

Her brain wanted to tell her it was simply because of his body heat, but her heart said something else.

Her heart said that the warmth was his feelings for her.

Hayley wanted to believe her heart, but she was a woman who lived in her head and not with her heart. She thought things through, she was sensible and smart, and always making lists to weigh out the pros and cons of each decision she had to make so that she could make a logical and informed choice.

She didn't let her emotions control her, maybe because as a child she had been overly emotional, crying over the smallest of things and clinging to her older sisters because the man who called himself her father terrified her. She had tried so hard to get a grip on her over sensitivity, but maybe she had gone too far. Maybe she had let her head override her heart, and that was why she hadn't told Brian how she felt about him. If she did and he turned her down then she was afraid that overemotionalness would come back and her heart would be shattered into a million pieces.

But standing here, with Brian's hand over her heart and hers over his, somehow, she felt like everything would be okay.

Somehow, she just knew that Brian would never hurt her.

They were friends. He'd been there all throughout her childhood—the good part of it anyway—they'd spent vacations and holidays, and just regular rainy weekends together. They knew each other, what they liked and disliked, they knew they had fun together, they knew they made each other laugh, and built each other up.

That was what real love was built on, right?

"You feel it don't you?" Brian asked, tenderly brushing the back of his knuckles across her cheek, then cupping the back of her head in his hand.

So overcome by emotion, Hayley couldn't speak, she just nodded. Brian began to shimmer as her eyes grew watery. You couldn't not cry when your dreams had finally come true.

"You're crying," Brian said, dismayed, catching a stray tear with the pad of his thumb as it wound its way down her cheek. "Hayley, you don't have to worry. Yes, what's happened the last few days made me realize what was in my heart, but it didn't make me fall for you. Just made me see what was already there. I've been falling for you for months now. This just forced me to accept it, to admit that I wasn't just attracted to you because you're beautiful but that I'm falling in love with you."

Falling in love.

Even though her head still wanted to fight against what Brian was saying, her heart believed it. Her heart *felt* it. She was already in love with Brian while he was still moving toward the same place, but he *was* moving there.

Hayley looked up, her eyes still watery, but they were happy tears not sad ones. Although she wasn't usually forward with men, she reached up, curled her hands around Brian's cheeks, and drew his face down to meet hers.

The kiss was soft, light, and unassuming as they took that first step out of the friend zone and into the couple one. Just like she could sense Brian's feelings for her, she could also sense his nervousness. They were both anxious about the changes that were happening in their relationship, but those changes were happening whether they acknowledged them or not. The more time she spent alone with Brian, the more her feelings grew, and she knew it was the same for him. It helped her to know that he was just as nervous as she was. It was reassuring, they were in this together, and if Brian was anxious it was because he wanted this to work out as much as she did.

~

6:29 P.M.

Brian could do this all day.

Just stand here and kiss Hayley. His hand was still on her heart, feeling it race beneath his touch, his other curled behind her head, drawing her closer as he took the kiss from gentle to deeper, more sensual.

At first, she had been hesitant to believe him when he'd said that he was falling for her. She didn't want to get her hopes up, he got that, but she didn't have anything to worry about. While it was true she had been in love with him a whole lot longer than he'd had feelings for her, he knew what he felt was real. That feeling of panic when he'd realized that if Hayley had died in that fire a part of him would be lost forever had been the wakeup call he'd needed to admit that he no longer saw Hayley as his little friend, but as someone he could see himself having a future with.

Only because his lungs were screaming for air did Brian break the kiss. Breathing heavily, he stared into Hayley's blue eyes as she stared—also breathing heavily—into his.

"This is odd," she said with a giggle.

"Good odd, I hope."

"*Very* good." She gave a contented sigh.

"Well, there's no going back now. After that kiss, I don't think I could go back to just being your friend."

"Good because I don't want you to," Hayley told him.

She still looked nervous, and he certainly still felt anxious. As much as he wanted to take things to the bedroom, Brian didn't think either of them was ready for that yet.

"Come and sit down." He took her hand and led her back to the couch. He knew what he wanted to say, but he didn't know how to say it. Brian wasn't used to being nervous around a woman. He'd dated off and on since he was in high school, but it had never gotten super serious because he hadn't been able to envision a future with any of those women.

But with Hayley, he saw it all.

He *wanted* it all.

He wanted marriage and kids and pets and a home. He wanted to have her by his side as he grew old. He wanted to share every day of the rest of his life with her.

But how could he say that now?

They'd been a couple—which he guessed they were now. That kiss certainly felt like it sealed the deal—for all of ten minutes if that. He couldn't just say that he wanted all of that. He didn't want to scare her off.

Although she was thinking the same things as he was, right?

She'd said that she'd had a crush on him since she was nine, so it made sense that Hayley wanted those same things as well.

"You look thoughtful," Hayley said, breaking his concentration.

"Just thinking about us."

"*Are* we an us? I mean, that kiss was … amazing … but does it mean that we're, you know, a couple?"

Since he knew that Hayley needed to hear it said out loud, he didn't beat around the bush. "Yes. As far as I'm concerned it means we're a couple."

As soon as he said the words, he felt her relax. "I've waited a really long to hear you say that. I didn't think I ever would."

There was no point in hashing out why she hadn't said anything about her crush, or he hadn't told her that he knew she had a crush on him, it wasn't important. What was important was that now both their feelings were out in the open, acknowledged, real, and they could start moving forward.

"I guess Jay Turner turned out to be good for something," he said, tucking her hair behind her ear, trailing his fingers down her slender neck, and settling them on her shoulder. "If he hadn't decided to blame you for taking Kinsley then I might not have realized just how deep my feelings for you ran."

"Sometimes things just have a way of working out for the best. Even the bad things."

As much as he knew Hayley was happy—thrilled—for them to finally be a couple he could feel that she was still tense. One good thing couldn't erase all the stresses of the last few days.

"Lie down," he instructed, standing up.

"What?" Hayley's brow furrowed in confusion.

"You look like you need a massage."

"A massage?" She arched a brow, her lips quirked up into a smirk.

"Hey, these hands that you were just complimenting aren't just good at playing Operation," he said, holding up his hands and grinning at her. This was why he could envision a future with Hayley when he couldn't with any of the other sweet, pretty, kind women he had dated before. They were friends, real friends, that had fun together, and this awkwardness of crossing out of the friend zone aside, they were comfortable together. That was the kind of foundation he wanted to build a life on.

"Okay," Hayley agreed, stretching out on her stomach on the couch, her long dark hair fanned out across her back and down over the side of the sofa like a waterfall in the dark.

"Beautiful," he murmured under his breath as he perched beside her.

"What did you say?"

"Nothing," he said because he knew Hayley didn't see herself the same way that others did. It wasn't that she was self-conscious about her looks, nor was she vain. She didn't wear a lot of makeup, just enough to highlight her already long lashes and large eyes and accentuate her plump lips, and she didn't spend a lot of time on her hair, usually leaving it hanging loose. She was stunning, but she didn't let it define her. It was one of the things he loved about her, and he knew that she wouldn't want constant compliments on her appearance.

"Liar." She giggled.

"I was just saying that you were beautiful, and don't go disagreeing," he added when she took a breath and was about to speak. Hayley kept her mouth shut, and he started to knead her shoulders, she was even tenser than he'd thought. Knowing she was sore and bruised from the events of the last few days, Brian kept his touch gentle while still giving her muscles a good working over, getting rid of the tightness and the kinks.

"Ahh, that's so good," Hayley sighed contentedly again and settled deeper into the couch cushions.

"I know what would make it better," he said.

"Oh yeah?" she asked, sounding a little suspicious.

As well she should. "Why don't you take off your sweater? It'll give me better access."

"Better access?" Hayley propped herself up on one elbow, amusement dancing in her eyes. "To what?"

"You. All of you."

Although her cheeks pinked in that adorable way they always did when she was anxious or embarrassed, she pulled her sweater up over her head and dropped it on the floor beside them, leaving her in just a pair of sweatpants and a simple white cotton bra.

"Brian?"

"Yeah?"

"You're staring."

"Oh, yeah."

She laughed, but it was a nervous laugh, and to put her back at ease, Brian leaned over and kissed her lightly on the lips, then put his hands on her shoulders and eased her back down so she was lying on her stomach again. Beginning at her shoulders, he massaged his way down her body, working the back of her neck and then down her spine. Skipping her backside and legs, he jumped down to her feet, rubbing them from heel to toe.

"These socks really should go too," he said, pulling them off her feet and tossing them down to join her sweater.

"Uh-huh," Hayley mumbled.

Moving on to her calves, he massaged them for a minute before pausing, wondering just how far he could push his luck. "You know ..." he said slowly.

"I think I can guess where this is going."

"These pants are a little in the way," he teased. "They should probably go as well."

"So, I'd be in my underwear, and you'd be fully dressed."

"I can fix that." Brian pulled his own sweater off and added it to the growing pile of clothes on the floor. Since Hayley hadn't protested the idea, he tugged her sweatpants down her legs, then eased her over onto her back so he could see her properly.

Even though she didn't work out a lot, Hayley's body was perfectly toned, her legs were long and slim, and her stomach was flat and smooth. Add that to her sky-blue eyes and the very light dusting of freckles across her nose and he could stare at her forever and never get tired of the view.

"This is why you wanted to undress me, to stare at me?" Hayley asked with a grin.

"Nope, I had something else in mind. If you want to," he added. There would definitely be no going back after this.

"I want to," she said without hesitation.

Removing the last of his clothes, Brian sat down beside her and took hold of her hips, lifting her onto his lap. Like they had done this a million times before instead of this being their first time, their lips found each other's, and his hands began to knead her bottom.

The kiss deepened, emotions passed between them, his fingers found their way inside her, and she moaned into his mouth. She began to rock against his hand as he worked her up, teasing her by moving faster then slowing right back down again.

"Brian," she whimpered. "I don't want to come until you're inside me."

Taking pity on her since he wanted their first time to be perfect, he reclaimed his grip on her hips and maneuvered her up and then lowered her down, so he slid inside her, buried deep.

Friendship had cemented their bond, and they moved in sync as they worked each other higher and higher. Hayley's nails dug into his shoulders and his into her bottom as they continued to move, faster and faster, with more and more urgency until they both toppled over the edge together.

"That was ... indescribable," Hayley panted, resting her forehead against his.

"It was pretty amazing," he agreed, wrapping an arm around her waist and pulling out of her as he turned her around and settled her in his lap.

"We didn't use a condom," Hayley said as she snuggled closer.

Brian reached for a blanket and tucked it around them. That was sloppy on his part. He'd been too eager to get inside her to stop and think of anything else. "No, we didn't."

"It's not really the best time for us to get pregnant. We only just started dating, we don't even know if we're going to make a good couple."

"I love kids, you love kids, we both want kids, we both know that we're going to make a great couple. If we just made a baby then we'll deal with it, but usually it takes more than just one time."

"You really feel that way?"

"With you? Absolutely. I already know we're going to spend the rest of our lives together, whether we start our family today, or a year from now, or ten years from now, I don't care. All I want is you."

# CHAPTER
## *Five*

December 23rd
9:17 A.M.

"I can't believe we spent the whole night down here," Hayley said, stretching. She'd never felt this good or this relaxed in her entire life. "You wouldn't have thought sleeping on the couch would be this comfortable."

"It's not like we did a whole lot of sleeping," Brian said, nuzzling her neck.

That was true. They'd made love—several times—explored each other's bodies and laid curled up in each other's arms talking. It was as close to perfection as a night could possibly be.

It still didn't feel real.

For pretty much as long as she could remember she had wanted this. Her feelings had gone from a childish crush on an older guy, to unrequited love that she had been sure would remain unrequited for the rest of her life, to finally having the man she loved love her back.

She wanted to stay here forever, in this special little bubble, where nothing else existed but the two of them. They could talk some more, sharing some of the personal things that you only shared with the person you loved, and make love a few more times.

This was perfect.

But she knew that perfection was always an illusion.

One that never lasted.

As amazing as last night had been, it didn't change the fact that Jay Turner was still out there somewhere and that he still wanted her dead. It didn't change the fact that he could go after another person she loved, or his daughter or wife.

Brian's hand moved from her shoulder where he had been lightly massaging her now totally relaxed muscles, and trailed down her arm, over her hip, and settled back between her legs.

"I could really get used to this," she said as he began to very gently stroke her.

"The sex is pretty awesome."

"I meant the massages," she teased.

"Oh yeah, how's this for a massage." Brian's fingers were like magic, and it wasn't long before she was moaning, whimpering, and squirming, trying to get him to increase the pressure as he moved impossibly slowly, drawing things out for her as long as he could.

Eventually, he took mercy on her, increased the pressure and speed, and sent her flying over the edge into indescribable bliss.

"That was better than any massage," Brian said smugly.

She would agree if she could talk, but she couldn't, she was still hovering in that zone where her mind and body hadn't quite reconnected yet.

Hayley had already curled her fingers around his impressive length, ready to return the favor when the doorbell rang.

Just like that, she was snapped out of her happy little bubble.

"Who could that be?" she asked—possibly in a borderline hysterical tone—as she scrambled out from under the blanket and off the couch.

"Let's just—"

She cut Brian off, too scared to be able to listen to anything. "No one but Ryan and Brady know that we're here. And they're supposed to call if something happens not just turn up here. Something must be wrong, right? Why else would someone be here? Do you think he went after my sister again? Or my mom or dad? Or maybe he managed to get to Kinsley. You don't think he hurt Sawyer, do you?"

"What I think is that we should probably just open the door and find out," Brian said with a calm she had no hope of matching.

"Right." She nodded a little too vigorously, hurting her neck in the process.

"Uh, Hayley," Brian said as she hurried to the door.

"What?"

"You might want to put some clothes on," he said with an amused smile as he looked her over from head to feet.

She followed his gaze and saw that she was still naked.

She'd forgotten.

She was too scared to think properly right now. She wasn't even sure she was capable of remembering how to put on her clothes.

As though sensing her quickly growing panic, Brian picked up her sweatpants and sweater and brought them to her, gently easing the sweater over her head, then taking her hands and sliding them through the sleeves.

"Hold onto my shoulders," he said as he knelt down.

She did, and he took hold of one of her ankles, slid the pants up one leg, and then repeated the process with the other.

He was so sweet.

As amazing as the hot sex had been, this was why she loved Brian because he genuinely cared about people and wanted to help them.

"Thank you," she said when he stood.

"Anytime." He leaned down and tenderly kissed her forehead.

Hayley waited for Brian to shrug into his clothes, then waited for him to join her at the door. She knew the drill, he was the bodyguard, and thus he was the one who opened the door, but it didn't mean she wasn't going to be right behind him waiting to find out what had happened.

"What took so long?" Arianna demanded when Brian finally got the door open.

"Ari?" Hayley asked, confused. Her sister looked fine as did Brady and Aurora Crowley and their twenty-one-month-old daughter Star.

"What's going on?" Brian asked, ushering everyone into the apartment and closing and locking the door behind them.

"Nothing," Brady replied. "Arianna is staying with us until the cops get Jay Turner in custody, and she wanted to come by. We thought you might feel a little un-Christmassy here without a tree, so we decided to bring you one and stop by for a visit."

"What if he followed you here?" Brian demanded, probably a little more forcefully than he should have, considering he was talking to his boss.

Brady rolled his eyes. "As if I was stupid enough to let him follow us. Even if he did know about us, and even if he did know Ari was staying with us, and even if he did find out where we lived, and even if he did know that we were coming to the safehouse, and even if he did try to follow us, do you really think I wouldn't have noticed?"

"Point taken," Brian acknowledged.

He might be ready to accept Brady and Aurora bringing Arianna here, but she certainly wasn't. "Why did you bring my sister here? What if he did somehow manage to follow you? What if he knows Ari is staying with you? What if he goes after her again?"

"I'm fine, Hales, don't worry." Arianna shot her a wide smile, but Hayley saw the hint of fear lurking deep in her sister's blue eyes.

"Really, Hayley," Brady added, "everything is fine. I won't let that man hurt your sister, I promise. I'm watching out for her just the same way I would for Aurora or Star."

"Cookie, Mama," the toddler said, pointing to the box in her mother's other hand.

"We didn't just bring your sister and a Christmas tree, we also have cookies," Aurora said with a smile intended to smooth things over.

Hayley let out a long, controlled breath.

She supposed everyone was right.

No one would be able to tail Brady without his knowing, and she was glad that the couple had opened their home to her sister until this whole mess was sorted out, especially considering they had a little girl to worry about.

"Cookie, Mama," Star said again, a little more forcefully, and she tried to squirm on her mother's hip to get to the box of cookies.

Hayley couldn't help but smile at the sweet little girl.

"Okay, I guess it's nice that you came. I *was* missing having a Christmas tree, and I *do* love cookies," she admitted.

"See, it was a good thing we came over." Arianna beamed and came to give her a hug. Hayley squeezed her sister tightly and held on a little longer than was necessary for a hug. She was so unbelievably glad Ari was okay. If Jay Turner had managed to get her into his van, she never would have forgiven herself. As it was, she was struggling to.

"So, Christmas tree or cookies first?" Brady asked as he set the tree he'd carried with him down on the floor.

"Cookies," Star screeched, her little face red, her fingers curled into fists.

They all laughed. "Cookies it is," Aurora said, setting her daughter down and opening the cookie box, giving one to Star.

"Where do you want the tree?" Brady asked.

"Over there," she and Brian said simultaneously. Hayley shot him a grin. Even in things like this they were in perfect agreement.

"Did you bring decorations?" Hayley asked as she followed Brady over to the corner on the far side of the room where he was starting to set up the tree.

"Did we bring decorations?" Brady echoed with mock horror. "Darlin', we brought decorations, tinsel, garlands, the whole works."

Hayley couldn't deny she was becoming happier by the second that Arianna, Brady, Aurora, and Star had stopped by for a visit. Without any decorations in the apartment, it hadn't felt like Christmas, but now they could have their own little Christmas here even if she was stuck and wouldn't get to spend the holidays with her family.

"What goes on first?" Brian asked, opening the box of decorations the others had brought.

"Lights," she and Arianna said in unison.

Everyone laughed again, and she felt the tension that had built back up inside her when the doorbell rang begin to fade away. Spending the morning with her sister and friends would be fun, especially since they'd be decorating the tree, then maybe once they left she and Brian could make love again.

~

11:22 A.M.

Sawyer yawned as he watched the kids play.

Kinsley Turner was settling into the group home and was gaining some confidence. She had finally come out of her room and had spent the morning playing with another little girl her age. They'd played with a doll's house and then built a castle with big wooden blocks. They'd painted pictures, and now they were busy making cakes and cookies with play dough.

So far, Jay Turner hadn't turned up here, other than the day he'd waited for Hayley and followed her and Brian, running their car off the road. Sawyer was starting to think the man was smart enough to know that coming here was only going to lead to his arrest. He hoped Jay was found soon though, so they could all go back to their lives.

As much as he was settling in here, he missed his wife, his kids, and his own house. Ashley called every day, and he always spoke to his twins, but Jackson and Janelle were only fourteen months old and didn't really get the idea of a phone. He was pretty sure it freaked them out hearing their daddy's voice but being unable to see him. As soon as Ash put the phone to their ears, they went quiet, but he could hear them babbling away in the background when he and Ashley were talking. They'd tried video calling, too, but that seemed to freak out the kids even more, so he and Ash had video chatted after she'd put the twins to bed.

He was missing them though.

Forty-eight hours without hugging his kids or kissing his wife was a lot. This was the longest he had been away from the twins since they were born and the longest he had been away from his wife since they'd been married. He had worked bodyguard cases since he'd gotten married but no overnight ones. He'd mostly been doing private security work at events which meant that he was home each night, or more accurately in the early hours of the morning. He couldn't wait to go home.

"Sawyer."

"Yeah?" he asked as Kinsley and her little friend came running over. "What's up, girls?"

"We're hungry, are we allowed to have a snack?" Kinsley asked. Her little face was anxious like she wasn't altogether sure whether or not she was going to get in trouble for asking for some food. The other little girl looked even more afraid.

Sawyer hated that.

He hated that these children had been abused to the point that they were now afraid of the most simple and small things. He wondered if they would ever completely let go of their fear. He hoped that they could. Seeing the kids here at the group home had made him resolve to be an even better father to his own kids. Sawyer knew that he couldn't prevent them from being afraid, or stop them from getting hurt, or disappointed, or anything else, but he could be there, right beside them, to hold them when they were scared and wipe away their tears. His son and daughter were going to know without a shadow of a doubt that he loved them more than he could ever put into words.

"Sure, we can grab a snack. How about some fruit?" he asked as he took the children's hands and led them to the kitchen.

"Fruit?" Kinsley echoed, her nose scrunched up a little. "Can't we have a cookie?"

"It's going to be lunch in an hour. I think fruit now, and maybe you two can have cookies for an afternoon snack." Neither of the kids complained, and he almost backtracked and told the girls they could have whatever they wanted. They certainly deserved it. But right now, when their lives were in turmoil, what they needed most was structure and consistency. They needed rules and all the same things that other kids their age got at home. "What about if we make banana people."

"What are banana people?" Kinsley asked.

"Banana people are people we make with bananas for their bodies, and berries for their eyes, and maybe a watermelon skirt, apple arms, or apricot smiles," he explained. His kids were only toddlers, but they loved making banana people. It actually got them eating something other than cookies.

"Can we use pears for something?" the other little girl asked, her voice barely more than a whisper, her eyes fixed firmly on the ground.

"If there are some in the fridge we sure can," he said. "Hop up at the table, and I'll see what fruit we have."

The girls clambered onto chairs while he raided the fridge and the fruit bowl and grabbed some toothpicks they could use to attach the banana people's faces, arms, legs, and clothes.

"Okay, girls, we have strawberries, nectarines, apples, raspberries, oranges, and peaches. Oh, and, Becca, you're in luck, there were some pears in there too." Sawyer was just setting all the fruit down on the table when something caught his attention outside the kitchen window.

Immediately, his bodyguard senses kicked into high gear.

His gut was telling him that something was wrong.

Without letting his concerns show, he didn't want to worry the girls, he said, "Kinsley, Becca, could you two please go straight into the office, tell Mrs. Kingston that she needs to get all the kids and take them into the playroom." He hoped the woman would get the message that something was wrong and that as well as gathering the children into one place she would also call 911.

Neither of the girls argued or talked back. They both climbed off their chairs and hurried out of the room while he put his hand on the butt of his gun and unlocked the back door.

When he stepped outside, he didn't see anyone but sensed them.

Someone else was out here.

He hadn't seen anything more than a moving form through the window, but he was pretty sure it was Jay Turner.

That or one of the teenagers sneaking out, but he didn't think that was the case here. The older kids were allowed to do the same things as other kids their age, they had to make sure they told someone where they were going to be, and there was a curfew, but they were allowed to go to the mall, see a movie, or go to the park.

His gut said it wasn't one of the older kids out here.

Carefully he scanned the yard. It was a reasonable size. There were two swings, a slide, a sandbox, and a teeter-totter. There were also three large trees down by the back fence and a grassy area where the kids could toss around a Frisbee or kick a ball.

Since there weren't really very many places to hide, Sawyer headed toward the trees. If he didn't find anyone back here, he'd circle the house in case Jay Turner—or whoever was out here—had already gone around the side of the building. Hopefully, by then the cops would be here.

It wasn't that he didn't think he could handle this on his own. He was just afraid of what he would do to the man when he did find him. Jay had killed his daughter, beaten his wife, and tried on several occasions to kill one of his friends, he deserved a little of his own treatment.

And the man had been hard to catch so far, always seeming to manage to slip away.

Well not this time.

Sawyer circled behind the first of the three trees.

There was no one there.

He was so sure that he'd seen someone.

Had he just imagined it? He'd been on edge the last two days, determined to do whatever he could to make sure Jay Turner didn't kill another of his daughters. He was away from his family just a few days before Christmas and worrying that he wouldn't be home in time to be there when his kids left milk and cookies for Santa on Christmas Eve and opened their presents Christmas morning.

He was just turning around when something dropped on him.

Not something, some*one*.

Jay Turner.

The man must have climbed up into the tree and been hiding there waiting for the perfect time to pounce.

Sawyer wasn't letting that man get anywhere near Kinsley.

Fumbling for his gun, he almost managed to get it out when Jay slammed something into his head.

He saw stars.

The shadow above him began to move away.

Ignoring the pain in his head, he managed to pull out his gun, and doing his best to aim it while seeing double, he fired.

Sawyer had no idea whether or not he hit his target, but he heard sirens, and confident that at the very least Jay Turner wasn't going to get a chance to get to Kinsley, he rested his head back against the grass and closed his eyes.

∽

1:03 P.M.

Ashley set a file in the filing cabinet and closed the drawer. She loved when they finished a job, and could put the file away. There was just something about that sense of completion that gave her a little rush.

Yeah, she was that much of a geek.

It wasn't that she was OCD about everything. She just liked that little burst of adrenalin when she could tick off a completed task from a list. And these days with two toddlers at home, she didn't get to finish off a lot of jobs. Most of the time it was like spinning in a circle, barely treading water. Dirty dishes stacked up so there was almost enough to fill the dishwasher by the time a load was done, and she didn't even want to think about the laundry, that was just a losing battle. Then there was the mess of toys that littered the floor, her house was pretty much a disaster zone.

But work was different.

At work she had a bit more control over her environment, so she kept her desk spotless. And maybe the rest of the offices too.

When she and Sawyer officially became a couple, she had wondered if it would be weird the two of them working together as well as living together. It wasn't like they had the same roles at the firm they worked for, Sawyer did bodyguard and security work, and she was the reception-ist. Still, spending a lot of their days together as well as their evenings and weekends could have been a problem.

Thankfully, it hadn't turned out to be.

She loved spending all her time with Sawyer and now with their kids as well. She had missed him so much the last two days while he'd been working around the clock as little Kinsley Turner's bodyguard. As soon as she put the twins down tonight, she was going to call him, maybe even give him a little peek at what he was missing while spending his nights away from home.

Ashley was smiling as she sat back down at the computer and didn't notice when one of her bosses walked in.

"Hey, Ash," Brady said.

Immediately the smile faded from her lips. There was something in his tone that she didn't like. She got along well with her boss, she and his wife Aurora were great friends, and their kids were pretty close in age, Aurora's daughter was only seven months older, so they often got all the kids together for play dates.

"What's wrong?" she asked.

"Can you come into my office for a minute?"

Fear filled her.

She wasn't worried that she was about to be fired. Not only was she good friends with Brady and her other bosses, but she was good at her job, reliable, prompt, and smart. Had something happened down in the daycare? She loved being able to bring her kids to work with her and pop down in her lunch break to see them. It was so much better than putting them in daycare somewhere else where she wouldn't be able to see them all day long.

On shaky legs she stood and came out from behind her desk, crossing the room and following Brady into his office.

"Sit down," he said, pulling out a chair for her.

She did.

He perched on the desk in front of her.

Her anxiety rose quickly.

Something was wrong.

Really wrong.

"Now, there's no need to panic, okay?" Brady started.

Ashley shot to her feet. The only time anyone ever said that was when there was indeed something to panic about.

"I said there was no need to panic," Brady repeated as he stood as well and took hold of her shoulders, gently pushing her back down into her chair.

"If you don't tell me what's wrong in the next thirty seconds I'm going to explode," she warned Brady.

He gave her a small one-sided smile that actually went a little way to calming her down. If Brady was smiling, then things couldn't be *too* bad.

"Please," she begged.

"There was an incident at the group home where Kinsley Turner is staying."

And now she was back to full-on panic mode.

An incident.

At the place where her husband was working.

There was no doubt in her mind that Sawyer had been hurt.

"How bad?" She managed to force the words out of her throat that was quickly closing. She had only been this scared in her life once before. She had almost been killed by a serial killer a few years ago but managed to be saved before he strangled her. Determined he wasn't going to let a victim survive he had stalked her until he was able to make a second attempt on her life, coming far too close to killing her and two of her friends, including Brady's wife, Aurora.

Knowing someone wanted to kill you, that kind of terror was indescribable.

As was the fear of her husband or children being hurt.

"Not bad, Ash," Brady assured her. "Not bad at all. Sawyer is okay. Do you hear me? He's fine. He thought he saw someone outside, so he made sure that the staff got all the kids together in one place and called the cops. He went outside to investigate. Jay Turner must have climbed up a tree, assuming that we would have someone on his daughter, and wanted to draw them out, intending to incapacitate them, then he'd have free range to get to Kinsley. He jumped down, knocked Sawyer over, then hit him over the head. Sawyer was able to fire off a shot, he hit Jay, but the man managed to get away again. He's like a cat with nine lives," Brady muttered.

Her husband had been hit over the head.

Head injuries were serious so how okay could Sawyer be?

And Brady had said that Jay got away even though Sawyer had shot him. Her husband was a perfect shot, if he hadn't incapacitated or killed the man then it was because he couldn't.

Because he was hurt.

"Put your head between your knees. You look like you're going to pass out." Brady's hand pressed between her shoulders, pushing her head down. "I told you he's okay, Ash. He's okay," he said again, over-enunciating the words, presumably to try to get them to penetrate.

It wasn't his words that were going to convince her that her husband was okay.

Only seeing him could do that.

As if by magic, she heard the door to Brady's office open and footsteps cross the room.

"Ash?"

It was Sawyer's voice, and he sounded okay, but she was very afraid that her mind had snapped, and she had lost touch with reality and was now hallucinating.

"Is she okay?"

"I don't think she believes you're okay," Brady replied.

"Can I have a moment alone with her?"

"Of course. As long as you need."

Brady's hand lifted from between her shoulder blades, and then a moment later, someone knelt in front of her. A finger was hooked under her chin, and her face was tilted up.

Sawyer was before her.

There was a lump on the side of his head the size of a gold ball.

He was pale.

There were still faint traces of blood streaking down his cheeks.

He didn't say anything, just leaned in and touched the softest of kisses to her lips.

Before she even realized it, tears were flooding down her cheeks in a torrent. A sob built up in her chest and then came bursting out as she sunk forward into Sawyer's arms.

He took her weight and eased them both down to the floor, settling her in his lap. He stroked her hair, rubbed her back, and held her as she wept.

"I'm sorry," she hiccupped at last when her tears started to dry up. "You were hurt and I'm crying all over you."

"Don't be sorry. Holding you in my arms was all I've wanted to do since it happened."

"Are you really okay?" Ashley lifted her head from Sawyer's shoulder and stared into his eyes, seeking the truth.

"Really and truly okay aside from a headache, and even that is duller now that I took some painkillers."

"I love you so much." She took his face between her hands and kissed him again, deeper and more passionately this time like it was the last time she would ever kiss him.

His tongue pressed between her lips, and one of his hands dropped to her bottom, kneading one of her cheeks.

"Sawyer," she said, breaking the kiss and putting her hands on his shoulders, lightly pushing him away. "What are you doing? We cannot have sex in our boss' office. Brady is right outside."

"Oh, I don't want to have sex in Brady's office," Sawyer said, standing and bringing her up with him. "Brady said to take the rest of the day off. Let's pick up the kids, go home, put them down for their naps, and then we're making up for the last two days of being apart."

Ashley couldn't think up a single argument against that.

It sounded perfect.

4:43 P.M.

"What do you want for dinner?"

Hayley laughed. "Dinner? You're thinking about dinner already? It's only quarter to five."

"I like to look forward to dinner, it's my favorite meal of the day." Brian grinned, his blue eyes sparkling.

For some reason he seemed to look extra hot this afternoon.

Maybe it wasn't anything different about him, but just her that was different.

She'd had such a wonderful twenty-four hours. The beginning of her and Brian's relationship as a couple and not just friends, making love all night, talking, learning things about him that she'd never known before, and sharing things about herself she'd never really verbalized even to herself. Then today hanging out with Brady and Aurora and her sister, they'd had so much fun decorating the little Christmas tree, laughing and talking, and watching little Star zoom around the apartment giggling and begging for more and more Christmas cookies.

It really felt now that she and Brian were a couple.

They hadn't worked out all the details, like if they were going to tell their families right away or wait until they'd been dating a while. Their families would be thrilled but it would kind of add pressure to their fledgling relationship because they wouldn't want to let everyone down. She didn't know how fast they were going to move. If they would take things slow or if they would talk about maybe moving in together when this was over, and they could go home.

But what she did know was that she was one lucky lady. As much as she'd miss her family if they had to spend Christmas here it would be kind of fun, just her and Brian, laughing, talking, drinking hot chocolate, eating turkey, exchanging gifts, watching Christmas movies, maybe they'd even put on some Christmas music and dance. And she already knew how the day would end. The two of them in bed together.

"What are you smiling about?" Brian asked.

"Nothing," she said, but she knew her cheeks were heating up, and that would tell him exactly what she had been thinking about.

"You're thinking about the two of us having sex again, aren't you?" Brian teased, his grin growing bigger. He leaned over and brushed his lips across her neck, making her shiver that delightful shiver Brian was so good at giving her. Then he took her hand and entwined their fingers. "I can't wait to tell our families. I don't think they're going to be surprised."

"My mom won't be, she's known about my crush since I was a teenager. She thought when we were older we would make a great couple."

"I'm pretty sure my parents think the same thing."

For now, she was glad they didn't have to make any decisions about their relationship beyond enjoying being in their own little bubble where they could just enjoy each other.

"So ..." Brian started, "did you decide what you wanted for dinner?"

Hayley laughed again. She loved this, just hanging out with her friend who was now her boyfriend, he made her laugh like no one else could. The downside to being a serious person was you didn't laugh a lot. It wasn't that she didn't have a sense of humor or that she was a negative or pessimistic person, it was just that she didn't often relax and let go. But with Brian it was so easy. She didn't have to worry about slipping back into old habits and being overly emotional, so that removed some of the pressure she put on herself, and she could just be her. The her she might have been if her start in life was normal.

"What about we steam some vegetables? And I thought I saw some chicken in the fridge. I know an awesome sauce we can make for it," she suggested. Hayley liked to cook but living alone she didn't usually bother to make much, it was too much work for only one person.

"Sounds perfect, then let's make homemade pretzels for dessert. I haven't made those since I was a kid, but we used to make them every Christmas and eat them on Christmas Eve while we watched Christmas movies."

"Sure, sounds fun. Then after dinner we can turn off the lights, turn on the Christmas tree lights, snuggle under a blanket with hot chocolate and the pretzels and watch all those old Christmas movies. Santa Claus is Coming to Town, Frosty the Snowman, Rudolph the Red-Nosed Reindeer, I love all those old movies."

"You're adorable." Brian kissed the tip of her nose then stood and headed to the kitchen.

Hayley stood, intending to follow him, but her phone buzzed with a new Facebook message. They'd brought their phones with them, although the location services and GPS tracking had been temporarily disabled, and they couldn't use them to call or message family.

Without thinking she picked it up, then almost dropped it again when she saw who the message was from.

"Brian."

The tone in her voice had him rushing to her side. "What's wrong?"

"Maria Turner just Facebook messaged me," she told him.

"What did she say?"

She hadn't even read the message yet. Putting in her passcode, she opened the messenger app and then the message from Maria. "She said she wants to talk to me about her husband. Do you think she's finally ready to turn him in after what he tried to do today?" Brady, Aurora, and Arianna had left earlier this afternoon after Brady got a message telling him that Jay Turner had tried to break into the group home where Kinsley was staying, injuring Sawyer Watson in the process.

"Reply, don't give away anything about where we are, but ask her what she wants to tell you about him."

Typing in a message, immediately after she hit send, she saw the message had been read, and the little dots that said Maria was typing a reply popped up.

They waited in silence to see what the woman was going to say.

"Brian, did you see this?" Hayley held the phone so they could both read the reply that said Maria wanted to turn Jay in.

"Message her back and tell her to give you the address of where her husband is hiding out so you can pass it on to Adam and Jessica."

Hayley typed that in, and then they both waited to see what Maria would say.

"She says she wants me to call her," she read the reply, even though she knew that Brian was reading it too.

"I don't like that," he said.

"This is what we've been waiting for," she protested.

"Tell her just to keep messaging."

"It's easier to talk to her. I feel like I have a better chance of convincing her she's doing the right thing if we're talking, I don't want her to back out. Jay isn't going to stop until I'm dead and he has Kinsley back. I don't want him to hurt that sweet little girl."

Brian exhaled slowly. "Fine, but call on one of the burner phones then we immediately turn it off."

She knew Brian didn't really want her to do this, but he also knew that this could be the only way they could end this before anyone else got hurt. She typed back asking for Maria's phone number, and the woman replied with it right away.

When Brian gave her one of the phones, she dialed, then waited nervously for the other woman to answer. She didn't want to mess this up.

"Hello. Maria?"

"Hayley?"

"It's me. I'm so glad you decided to do this. It's the right thing to do."

"I don't want Jay to hurt Kinsley."

"I know you don't. You love your daughter. If you give me the address, I'll call Adam and Jessica and have them go and pick him right up. Or I can have them go to your house, and you can tell them the address."

"No," came the emphatic reply.

"What do you mean, no?" She exchanged a glance with Brian who was leaning over her shoulder to listen in on the call and looked just as confused as she felt.

"I ... I don't trust them," Maria stammered. "I don't want Jay to get hurt. I just can't let him hurt Kinsley. What if ... couldn't you ...?"

"Couldn't I what?" she asked when the woman didn't continue.

"Could you come here?"

"Come where?"

"To my house. I don't want to talk to the cops. They just want to arrest Jay, they don't care about Kinsley."

Hayley knew that wasn't true, but she wasn't going to argue about it. "I suppose I can go to your house." Hayley felt Brian tense beside her, but she ignored him. Right now, getting Maria to tell them where her husband was hiding out was her number one priority.

"You care about Kinsley I know you do. You really want to make sure she's safe. I want to as well, but I'm scared. Jay is ... well, he's got a temper, especially when he drinks, and I ... I ... I'm not sure I can do this. But you, you're so strong, I don't want to talk to anyone else, only you. I don't think I can do this without you."

"And you don't have to," she assured the other woman.

Hayley couldn't imagine living the life Maria had. Her parents had loved one another, her dad had never laid a hand on her mom or on her and her sister, and she knew Brian would never do anything to hurt her. She wanted Maria to know that she didn't have to be afraid of her husband anymore. She wanted the woman to realize that she was worth more than what Jay had convinced her she was. She wanted Maria and Kinsley to have a happy life and a future where they could be and do anything they wanted.

The only way to do that was to take Jay out of the equation.

"I'm on my way."

∾

5:21 P.M.

"I don't like this."

"Everything will be fine," Hayley said.

She'd said that already.

Several times.

And yet Brian couldn't shake the feeling that things weren't going to be fine.

They were in his car on the way to Maria Turner's house. They'd called Adam and Jessica to make sure the cops would meet them there, and he'd also called Brady because he wanted to have backup. Taking Hayley out of the safehouse felt like a mistake. She was safe there, Jay had no idea where they were, and since no one besides Brady and Ryan knew, there wasn't much chance he would find out.

But out here they were like sitting ducks.

"It's getting dark," he muttered under his breath.

"It's winter," Hayley reminded him. "We're lucky there's this much light."

That was true. Although it was almost five-thirty, there was still the last lingering daylight, only because it had been a clear day and the clouds had stayed away meaning the last rays of the sun still touched the horizon. That wouldn't last long though, they were still fifteen minutes away from the Turner house, and by the time they got there it would be pitch black out. There were streetlights and the lights from houses decorated for the holidays, but it wasn't enough. It felt like they were going into this blind, and he already felt like Maria had the upper hand.

"Brian, you don't need to worry," Hayley said, reaching over and covering one of his hands. It was tightly clutching the steering wheel as though that would somehow give him the reassurance that he needed. Hayley's slender fingers curled around his, gently loosening his death grip.

"I don't like this," he said again.

"You can keep saying that, but it's not going to change anything. You're here, you're not going to let anything happen to me. Brady,

Adam, and Jessica are on their way to the house. What is going to happen with two cops, one ex-cop turned bodyguard, and you there?"

He was touched by her confidence in him, but it didn't change the facts.

Someone wanted Hayley dead, and he had just taken her out of the one place she was actually safe.

Brady, Adam, and Jessica had all agreed that this was their best move. Possibly their only move if they wanted to end this quickly. None of them believed they were bringing Hayley into a situation where she would be in danger.

None of them except him.

"We're just going to talk to Maria," Hayley continued. "She just needs a little reassurance. She wants to do the right thing for herself and her little girl, but she's scared, the hold that Jay has on her is tight, but she's trying to shake it off. As soon as she gives us the address of where Jay is hiding out, you and Brady will take me to the police station and Adam and Jessica will go and arrest Jay. Then this will all be over. We can go home, tell our families about us, and then celebrate Christmas with the people we love. Everything is going to work out just fine, there really isn't any need for you to worry."

He wished he had even an ounce of Hayley's optimism.

Because he didn't want to worry Hayley, they needed her calm so she could get out of Maria Turner what they needed. He forced himself to relax, at least outwardly. He took Hayley's hand, lifted it to his lips, kissed the back of it then set their joined hands on his thigh.

"I guess you're right," he said. "This is the best way to end this, I just don't like it."

"You don't have to. You just have to be here with me."

Brian had to admit he loved Hayley's fierce determination to do what she thought was the right thing. As worried as he was about her, he was also pretty damn proud. She was the one whose life was in danger, yet all she could think about was doing what she had to to make sure that little Kinsley Turner was safe.

How could you not love a woman like that?

"I *am* here with you, always," he promised. There wasn't anything that would tear him away from her side.

"I know." She squeezed his fingers tightly, letting him know just how much his support meant to her.

Adam and Jessica were already at the Turner house. As far as they could tell, Jay wasn't there. Cops had been posted on the house since Jay ran, and they hadn't seen him come back, so he knew they weren't walking into a trap, and yet still this feeling just wouldn't go away.

Maybe if he stopped focusing on the next hour or so and on what would happen after he'd start feeling better. As soon as Jay was in police custody they could go home. Part of him was a little sad about that. He'd gotten used to having Hayley around twenty-four-seven and he didn't really want to see it end.

"So ..." he said slowly.

"So, what?" Hayley asked with a smile.

"I was just wondering, once Adam and Jessica arrest Jay and we go home, I was wondering if maybe you wanted to come and stay with me?" Brian held his breath as he waited for her answer.

She took her time giving it.

Seconds ticked by into a minute and still she hadn't said anything.

"You really want me to move in with you?"

"Of course."

"What, like permanently?"

"Yes."

"So, you want the two of us to live together?"

"Uh-huh."

"Even though we've only been a couple for twenty-four hours."

"Well technically, but it's not like we don't know each other." If she wasn't ready, he would respect that. They'd live in their own places, have the occasional sleepover, he'd go to her house to pick her up for dates, and spend every spare second he had with her. But going to sleep each night with her in his arms and waking up each morning with her curled up beside him would be amazing.

He turned into the street the Turner house was located on. They only had four blocks to go before they got there and waited to hear Hayley's response.

She drew in a long, slow breath, he could practically hear her mind ticking over.

"I think that—"

Hayley never got a chance to finish her sentence.

A car rammed into them on his side.

Brian lost control of the car.

It spun wildly across the road, which was luckily empty.

Everything seemed to move in slow motion.

The car turned in a circle.

Hayley screamed.

He fought the steering wheel.

They connected with a pole.

Pain splintered through his body.

His head bounced into the airbag—which deployed as the car hit the pole—and then snapped back into the headrest.

He saw stars.

Blackness brushed the edges of his mind, trying to soak into the rest of it.

He fought against it.

Hayley was quiet.

Brian turned his head.

Cursed at the resulting pain.

Kept turning it anyway.

Saw Hayley lying slumped, unmoving, in her seat, held in place only by her seatbelt.

Had he been distracted?

Not seen another car coming until it was too late?

Or was this another ambush by Jay Turner?

It couldn't be.

Could it?

How would Jay know they were coming?

Maria was going to turn him in. He thought he had his wife completely under his thumb, there was no way he would expect her to do that.

It was dark now.

The Christmas lights of the nearby houses were blinding him.

Where was his gun?

He needed his gun.

He had to protect Hayley.

"Hayley," he croaked as he tried to fumble with his seatbelt to get it undone. He had to get to her. He had to see if she was okay.

Her car door was wrenched open.

Help.

It had to be help.

"Call an ambulance," he mumbled, or at least he hoped he did, but his pulse was drumming in his ears so loudly he could hardly hear anything else.

"We won't be needing an ambulance," a voice smirked.

He knew that voice.

It was Jay Turner.

"No, stop," Brian said as he tried once again to—unsuccessfully—undo his seatbelt. Where was his weapon?

There was rustling.

Moaning.

Then he thought he saw Hayley being dragged out of the car.

"I'm sorry," whispered a voice.

A female voice.

Not Jay's.

He thought it was Maria's.

Why was she here?

She was supposed to be waiting for them at her house.

Then it hit him.

She'd tricked them.

Lured them into a trap so her husband could get Hayley.

She'd been wrong. Maria wasn't strong enough to break the hold her husband had on her.

He had to get to her.

If he didn't, Jay would torture and kill her.

He couldn't let that happen.

He couldn't lose the woman he loved.

The car door was slammed shut.

The noise echoed inside his head, then threw him into unconsciousness.

~

5:33 P.M.

"Daddy, almost Christmas," Star said excitedly.

Brady smiled. He loved that his little girl was old enough this year to be excited about Christmas. She had been talking about it ever since they put up their Christmas tree on December 1st. And Star talked a lot. A lot. She had started talking a full month before her first birthday and hadn't stopped since. She wasn't even two years old yet, and she spoke in full sentences and could carry on a whole conversation. She started speaking the moment her eyes opened in the morning and didn't stop until they tucked her in.

Already he was dreading Star's teenage years.

His daughter wasn't anything like him—which was definitely a good thing—nor was she like her mother—although in looks she was definitely Aurora's mini-me. He was a mostly reformed bad boy with a death wish, and Aurora was the sweetest woman on the planet. Star was a little firecracker, she was loud, and outgoing, and was probably going to make him go gray before his time.

"I know, honey. I have to go to work now. Can you put Mommy back on? Goodnight, I love you, I'll come in and kiss you when I get home, but you'll probably be asleep already."

"Night, Daddy." Star blew him a kiss, then he heard shuffling as she obviously handed the phone off to her mother.

"Brady, what time do you think you'll be home?" Aurora asked.

"Hopefully not late, but probably not until after Star has gone down for the night. I'm almost to the Turner house, hopefully Hayley can convince Maria that she's doing the right thing, then Brian and I are going to take Hayley to the station while Jessica and Adam go and arrest Jay. Once they have him in custody, Hayley and Brian can go home, and I can come home to my two favorite girls." He couldn't wait to get home and celebrate Christmas with his family. Christmas Eve was the day he and Aurora had first met, and while it had been a shaky start, he was so glad he'd found her. She had brought light to his dark life, and he now felt like he was actually living instead of just waiting to die.

"I'll keep dinner warm for you, then you can help me wrap the last of the Christmas presents."

"Wrapping gifts is definitely your department." He chuckled. He wrapped his gifts for Aurora but wasn't very good at it. "*Un*wrapping is more my thing."

She laughed, getting his meaning without him having to say it. Over the last few years, he had definitely started to rub off on her. When they'd met she'd been borderline afraid of sex, now she was even confident enough to come onto him. "I can't wait. I may have a little surprise for you when you ..."

He stopped listening when he saw a truck come out of nowhere and slam into a car a couple of blocks ahead of him.

It wasn't an accident.

The truck had no headlights on.

It had been lying in wait.

"I have to go," he told Aurora. "I love you."

"Love you too," she said. She was used to him having to abruptly end phone calls while he was at work, and she didn't take offense to his brisk tone. She knew firsthand what he was like when he got into the work zone.

Pulling his car to the side of the road as he jumped out, he saw someone pulling a woman out of the passenger side of the car. Brady didn't even have to be able to see properly to know that this was Brian's car, that the apparently unconscious woman was Hayley, and the man from the truck was Jay Turner.

Gun in hand, he approached carefully.

"Let her go, Jay," he called out. All he could see were shadows, but when you spent most of your adult life living in the dark you learned to see shadows pretty well.

"I'm not walking away without her this time," came the snarled reply. "Maria, do it."

Maria was here too?

How had Jay gotten to Maria?

Had he hurt Jessica and Adam?

"Maria, you wanted to do the right thing," he called out to the shadowy figure that stepped out into the middle of the street, standing close to the mangled car. "Come over here by me, don't let him take Hayley. Once he has her, he's going to kill her, and then he's going to try to get Kinsley back. Don't let him hurt Kinsley like he did Leah."

Jay laughed, that kind of laugh you gave when you knew you had the upper hand. "Do it," he ordered.

A tiny speck of orangey red appeared where Maria was standing, a second later it dropped toward the ground, and then a larger flame burst up, moving slowly toward the wreck that had been Brian's car.

"The bodyguard is still in there." Jay laughed again, then climbed into the truck.

Brady had a choice, try to stop Jay from running with Hayley or get Brian out of the car before the line of fire hit it and blew it up.

When it came down to it there was no choice.

Hayley was in danger, but Jay wouldn't kill her right away, so there was time to find her. Brian would be dead in minutes if he didn't do something.

With a growl that came from hating being backed into a corner, Brady ran to the car as the truck took off down the street. Thankfully, Hayley's side of the car had taken the brunt of the impact and Brian's door appeared to be intact. He yanked on it, and it opened. Inside the car Brian was fighting—fairly uncoordinatedly—with his seatbelt.

Reaching over, Brady unsnapped the buckle, wrapped an arm around Brian's shoulders, and all but dragged him out of the car. Taking the other man with him, he ran from the car so they wouldn't get caught up in the inevitable explosion.

"Hayley," Brian muttered over and over, trying to stagger off in the direction the truck had gone.

"They're gone," he said. Rounding his SUV, he pushed Brian down and held him in place with one hand while he pulled his phone from his pocket and called in the cops and an ambulance. Then he called Adam and Jessica, he had to find out if they were okay. They would have noticed Jay breaking into the Turner house and kidnapping Maria, and yet neither of them had called to give him a heads up.

"Hello," Jessica said when she answered.

"Jay and Maria Turner just rammed Brian and Hayley's car with a truck, then abducted Hayley and tried to blow up the car with Brian still in it so I couldn't chase after them," he summarized.

"Is Brian okay?"

"I got him out before the—" he broke off as the car exploded behind them. "Before the car exploded."

"Adam and I have been sitting here waiting for you guys since Maria called Hayley and then Brian called us. We haven't seen any signs of Jay."

"Maybe he had already abducted Maria before she made the phone call. This whole thing could have been a trap intended to lure us in so he could get to Hayley. Since he didn't know where she was, he knew she wouldn't be able to resist doing anything to protect Kinsley. The truck didn't have any lights on, he was waiting for them."

"She was in on it."

"What?" He looked down at Brian, who had stopped struggling to get up on his feet and had sagged back against his SUV. "Who was in on what?"

"Maria." Brian looked up at him. While he looked like he was in pain his blue eyes were clear, it didn't appear he had a head injury that was impairing his judgment.

"What was Maria in on?"

"This." He waved a hand at the burning car. "In the car, when Jay was dragging Hayley out, she apologized to me. She didn't call Hayley because she wanted to turn Jay in, she called because she wanted to get us out of the safehouse so her husband could kidnap Hayley. And now he has. He's going to kill her."

Brady wanted to say something reassuring, but he didn't know what.

The facts were that Jay Turner did have Hayley and they knew for a fact that unless they could find her first, he was going to kill her.

"We still have time, don't give up hope just yet," he said. He knew it was lame, but it was the best he could do. "Did you hear that?" he asked Jessica who was still on the line.

"We did, we're coming. We can see the flames so we know where you are."

He hung up and stared at the burning car, they'd made a mistake.

All of them. They should have entertained the possibility that just because Maria had been abused by her husband didn't mean that she wasn't loyal to him or that she wasn't involved in this plan to kill Hayley. After all, she had lost both her daughters, just like Jay had.

Brady prayed Hayley wasn't going to pay the price for that mistake.

~

5:45 P.M.

"In and out, remember," Jay said.

"I know," Maria assured her husband. She knew what she had to do and was fully prepared to do it, no matter what.

"Don't mess up," he warned, his blue eyes shooting those familiar arrows at her.

She'd missed that.

She'd missed *him*.

She didn't care what anyone said. She didn't care what anyone thought about it, she loved her husband. She didn't care that Jay beat her, she didn't care that sometimes he used her in the bedroom so roughly that she could barely walk for days, she didn't care that he'd broken her bones and shed her blood, she loved him with her whole heart.

"I won't mess up," she promised.

Maria climbed out of the truck's cab as did Jay and followed him as he walked around to the back and opened it, shining a torch on Hayley Hood who lay inside. The woman didn't move, didn't indicate that she was aware of their presence, but she wasn't sure if it was just Hayley playing possum or whether the woman really was still unconscious.

"I think I'll spend a little time with our guest while we wait," Jay said. That familiar glint in his eyes, the curl of his lip, the way his forehead crinkled, all of it sent an arrow of jealousy through her.

She didn't want him laying a hand on Hayley Hood.

Those hands of his were hers, they should be on her body, they should be hurting her, wrapped around her neck, hitting her, making her scream.

"Are you pouting?" he growled in her ear.

"N-no," she said with a shudder. She was sure she had been, and she knew that meant he was going to punish her. She hoped he would. She needed him to. It had been days since she'd last seen him and the wounds he had inflicted had already begun to heal and no longer caused her much pain.

She needed it.

Pain was her drug of choice.

Without it, she felt like she was going to shrivel up and die.

"Come here," he ordered, wrapping a hand around her arm so tightly his fingers dug into her muscle, and she winced.

Jay dragged her up into the back of the truck and propped one foot up against the door, bending her over his knee, he yanked her skirt up, exposing her bare backside and slapped her five times in quick succession. Her skin stung, but it wasn't enough, she needed more. So much more.

"Now go," he said, roughly releasing her, causing her to stumble. "They know now that you're involved, even if they don't know to what extent, they might have already called and told the group home not to let you near Kinsley."

Maria nodded and climbed out of the truck. She wasn't going to let anyone keep her daughter away from her any longer. She was going to walk in there, ask to see her child, then grab Kinsley and run. If anyone tried to stop her then she was going to use the gun Jay had given her.

The street was clear of cop cars as she hurried further down the block and then down the path to the front door. She hoped they weren't hiding somewhere, she was ready to just get Kinsley and get out of here, start over somewhere else, somewhere where no one knew them, and no one knew what had happened to Leah.

She was shaking by the time she knocked on the door. Her hand brushed the gun hidden in the deep pockets of her jacket.

It felt like an eternity until the door was opened by an older woman with a pretty face and a huge mop of white curls.

"May I help you?"

"I'm Maria Turner. My little girl Kinsley is here. I was wondering ... could I please ... I just want ... I know I'm not supposed to ... I just want to tell her that I love her. Please," she added for extra emphasis. Technically, the cops and child protective services had removed Kinsley because of Jay who they believed had killed Leah, and not because of her, so she was hoping that the social workers might have pity on her and let her see Kinsley.

"I'm really not supposed to," the woman said, but her brown eyes were sympathetic, and she looked like she really wanted to say yes. It was the holidays, and she was no doubt saddened by the fact that a little girl wasn't at home with her family.

"Please. Just for a second. Could you call someone maybe? Ask for permission? The social worker assigned to the case is Hayley Hood, and the cops looking for my husband are Adam Abram and Jessica Spears."

"If a judge has already signed to say that Kinsley should be removed then you're not allowed to visit with her until you're granted visitation or it's deemed safe for her to return home."

Maria was losing her patience.

She wanted Kinsley back, and she knew that Jay was out in the truck with Hayley Hood, she wanted to get to them as quickly as she could. And the cops could come at any moment. They knew she had helped Jay kidnap Hayley. They could be worried that the two of them might try to come here and get their daughter.

"You'll have to leave, Mrs. Turner. The children are about to have their dinner, and I think it will be worse for Kinsley if she sees you here."

She was about to yank out her gun and demand that the woman bring her daughter, but fate was on her side, and all of a sudden, a group of about ten children came running down the stairs, Kinsley amongst them.

As soon as her daughter saw her, she came running over.

Maria snapped her arms around her little girl before the social worker had a chance to grab her.

Then she pulled out her gun. "I don't want to shoot anyone, but I will if you try to stop me."

A man with a gun had come down the stairs with the children. She wasn't going to hang around and find out if he was going to use it.

She turned and ran.

She heard voices and commotion behind her but didn't stop to find out what was going on.

The truck's engine was running, so she sped up and ran as fast as she could, shoving Kinsley in and jumping in after her.

"Shoot at them," Jay ordered.

As she always did when he told her to do something, Maria complied. Opening her window, she fired off several shots, and Jay took off down the street.

"Mama?"

Maria pasted on a smile as she looked down at her terrified little girl. "We're all together again. Isn't that nice?"

Kinsley looked from her to Jay and back again, then nodded.

Her daughter would learn.

Kinsley would learn the same lessons that life had taught her. She would learn that pain could be a beautiful thing when it came from the man you loved. Maria had learned that from her mother, whose husband used to beat her daily. The man wasn't her father, her father had split before she was born, but he was the man who had been her male role model growing up.

Those early experiences had taught her that the husband ruled the house with an iron fist, and it was the wife's job to cater to his every whim and attend to everything so he didn't have to. If you failed, you were punished. Could she help it if she enjoyed those punishments?

No, she could not.

Despite beating her mother daily, her stepfather had never laid a hand on her. The only person in her life to beat her was her husband.

One day Kinsley would find a husband of her own. And while her daughter had already had that first taste of pain from her father, it would be the man she loved who would show her just how precious pain could be.

"I don't think anyone is following us," Jay said.

"That's good." All she wanted was to get out of here and start their new lives. "Where are we going?"

"Back to where I've been staying," Jay answered. "We'll stay there for a few days, then once Hayley is dead and things have calmed down the three of us will leave."

She wanted to argue.

To say they should leave now. Staying was too risky. As it was, they would spend the rest of their lives looking over their shoulders.

But she didn't.

Because it wasn't her place.

Her place was to obediently do whatever her husband told her to, regardless of how she felt about it.

So, Maria settled Kinsley on her lap, put the seatbelt around them both, and then sat quietly waiting for her next directive.

# CHAPTER
## Six

December 24th
12:04 A.M.

"Why don't you go home, get some rest? I'll call you if we get something."

Brian just stared at Brady like he couldn't believe the man had just said that. Which he couldn't. He wasn't going home until he was taking Hayley with him.

"He's had Hayley for almost seven hours now," he said, picking at the edges of the bandage taped over a gash on his arm that had been deep enough to need stitches. "What do you think he's done to her already?"

"I don't think that's productive thinking," Brady replied.

"Well then tell me what I should be thinking about? I was Hayley's bodyguard. I knew that taking her out of the safehouse was a bad idea, but I let myself be talked into doing it anyway. I didn't notice the truck waiting to ambush us, I didn't stop them from taking her. We know what he wants to do to her, he wants to kill her, slowly, so that she suffers. That's not us guessing, or profiling, or anything like that, it's what we know he wants to do. He has her, alone, just him and his wife. He's hurting her. So what do you think he's doing to her?"

"I think obsessing over this isn't going to help," Brady said adamantly.

Not to be dissuaded from this conversation, Brian continued, "How long do you think until he kills her? I know he wants to drag it out, make her suffer, but he also knows we're onto him. I think he'll kill her quicker than he initially intended to."

"I agree with that assessment."

Brian nodded. He didn't really care if Brady agreed with him or not, he was just talking through what he was thinking because it was keeping him marginally sane.

Seven hours.

That was a long time to know that the woman you loved was in the hands of someone who hated her and wanted to punish and murder her.

After Brady had pulled him from the wreck of his car before it exploded, he'd been taken to the hospital, despite his insistence that he didn't need a doctor. His injuries weren't particularly serious, cuts, bruises, and a broken nose, nothing that had required a stay in the hospital.

Brady had followed the ambulance to the hospital, and as soon as he was finished being examined in the ER, he'd asked to be brought to the station where Adam and Jessica were working. His family had rallied—as they always did when one of their own was in trouble—but he hadn't wanted to sit around one of their houses as they waited for news.

Being around his family and Hayley's only added to his guilt.

How would he ever face them if they didn't get her back alive?

That was a very real possibility.

One that he had to start accepting and finding a way to come to terms with.

Jay Turner wanted Hayley.

Jay Turner had Hayley.

Jay Turner wasn't going to let this opportunity go to waste.

The cops hadn't been able to find Jay Turner.

The cops had no idea where Jay Turner had hidden himself away.

The cops had no way of finding Jay Turner.

Thus, the logical conclusion was that Jay Turner would kill Hayley before they could find him.

The sooner he learned to accept that the easier it would be. Only Brian knew that he would never be able to accept losing Hayley. She was a part of him now, she had been for a long time, he just hadn't seen it. The last twenty-four hours they'd spent together had been amazing. She had left a permanent mark on his soul that would never fade.

He loved Hayley.

After years of seeing her as just another little cousin, and then just an attractive friend, he now loved her so much that his heart was physically aching not having her here with him.

He didn't think he could live a lifetime with this pain.

"What are you thinking?" Brady asked.

His gaze snapped up to meet his friend's. "Thinking about what it's going to be like if we don't get Hayley back."

"We will get her back."

"You can't know that. She could be dead already. What would you do if you lost Aurora?"

"Rip out the heart of the person who took her away from me," Brady answered candidly, his dark eyes growing darker.

"Is that what you did to the men who tried to kill her?" He knew a little about the way Brady and Aurora had met, which was far from a conventional story.

"No, I beat them to a bloody pulp. And I would do the same to anyone who ever laid a hand on my wife or daughter."

Somehow Brady's calm but violent fury soothed him a little.

It gave him a purpose.

If he couldn't get Hayley back, he would make sure the man who had taken her from him suffered just like he had made Hayley suffer.

"How are you doing, Brian?" Adam asked as he and Jessica walked into the room.

Ignoring that, it mattered little at the moment, all that mattered was finding Hayley. "Did you ever find this Sarah person that Kinsley mentioned?" It wasn't just Hayley's life that hung in the balance now, but little Kinsley Turner's as well. After abducting Hayley, Jay and

Maria had gone straight to the group home where Maria had pulled a gun and used it to escape with her daughter.

"We found Sarah," Jessica replied.

"And?"

"And Jay Turner hasn't been hiding at her house," Jessica told him.

"How can you be so sure?" So far that seemed to have been the only lead the cops had in finding this violent man. How could they dismiss it so easily as a possibility?

"Because Sarah was a fifteen-year-old girl who lived across the street from the Turner's. We confirmed with her and her mother that she sometimes babysat Kinsley. Sarah lives in the house with her mother, stepfather, three siblings, and another three half-siblings. There is no way Jay Turner could have been hiding out there and no one know about it. Just to be sure, we spoke with Kinsley and asked her if that was the Sarah she was talking about, and she said it was. We also searched Sarah's house, Jay wasn't there. Wherever he's hiding it isn't there," Jessica summarized.

"So, if he isn't hiding at Sarah's house, then where is he?" Brian asked, frustrated. This was why he could never be a cop. He didn't have the patience to go through piece after piece of useless evidence trying to find the one little thing that would make the whole case click into place.

"Adam and I have gone through every person we could think of. Both of Jay's parents are deceased, no grandparents, an uncle who lives in France, his brother died in a drunk driving accident nearly four years ago, and we spoke with his sister who says she hasn't spoken to her brother since she turned eighteen and got out of their house."

"How can you be so sure of that?"

"We checked out the sister's place, and we've had cops on it ever since, no signs of Jay," Jessica explained.

"What about Maria's family?"

"Biological father split before she was born, stepfather is in the end stages of liver disease from a lifetime of alcoholism. Her mother is deceased, no siblings, and no other family. Wherever Jay Turner is hiding it isn't with a relative."

"You've been quiet," Brady said to Adam, who had taken a seat at the table in one of the conference rooms at the police precinct and not said a word since.

"I was thinking," Adam said slowly.

"About?" Brian asked.

"Well, we know that Maria Turner is involved. We're not sure to what extent, but we know at least she was involved in Hayley's abduction as well as Kinsley's. For all we know, she was also involved in Leah's death," Adam said. "We've been focusing most of our efforts on Jay and people connected to him, but so far that hasn't led us to anything useful. Once we found out that Maria was an active part of the ruse to get Hayley out of the safehouse, Jessica and I started looking into her past more closely."

"What did you find?" Brian was beginning to feel like they were never going to find Hayley. Just sitting around here wasn't doing anything. He would rather be out in his car just driving around looking for her. This was torture, and he wasn't sure he could endure it for much longer.

"Maria's mother was also abused by her alcoholic husband. At one point, Maria was briefly removed from her home, she was five years old at the time. When Jay tried to abduct Arianna, she said she smelled grandmother smells on him. Assuming that she's right and we are looking for an older woman, Jessica and I looked into the social worker who removed Maria from her home. The woman is now in her seventies, her name is Katherine Horton, she's retired, she's a widow, we're just trying to track down her address."

Hope flickered inside him.

Could this be it?

Could this be where Jay Turner was holed up with his wife, daughter, and Hayley?

Brian prayed that it was.

~

1:52 A.M.

. . .

Hayley wished he would just come back and do it already.

Sitting here waiting had to be worse than whatever Jay Turner had planned for her.

Right?

Only Hayley wasn't so sure she was right.

He'd beaten her in the back of the truck while Maria went to kidnap Kinsley, but since they'd arrived at this house, he hadn't come back to see her, just dumped her in a room with Kinsley, locked the door, and left.

Hayley suspected she knew what he was doing.

Jay was with Maria.

No doubt beating her.

For some reason she couldn't fathom, Maria liked being beaten basically into unconsciousness by her husband. Whatever psychological problems Maria had didn't excuse her behavior. She had been complicit in the abuse her daughters had suffered. She had been complicit in Leah's death—for all she knew Maria had been an active participant as well. She had been complicit in the plan to lure her out of the safehouse. Plus, she had abducted her own daughter.

Maria was just as guilty as her husband, and she would make sure that neither of them ever got Kinsley back. Well, she would if she could. But right now, she was Jay and Maria's prisoner, and they already had Kinsley. Once they killed her, they would flee with their daughter, and there would be nothing she could do about it.

"Hayley?" Kinsley said, wriggling so she was looking up at her.

The two of them were sitting on the floor of a bedroom in someone's house—not the Turner house but wherever Jay had been hiding out—one of her wrists was tied with rope to the metal frame of the bed, and her other arm was curled around Kinsley, holding the child close. "Yeah, honey?"

"I'm scared."

"I know, sweetie, so am I. Do you still have Brownie?"

"Uh-huh."

"Then you just hold him really tight, okay?"

"Okay."

She would do whatever she could to try to keep the child safe, but right now she didn't really like her chances. She'd hit her head in the car crash when Jay and Maria had rammed their car with a truck. She still had a headache, and the world was still a little blurry, so she was pretty sure she had a concussion. She had bumps and bruises over most of her body, both from the crash and from Jay punching and kicking her while they waited for Maria to kidnap Kinsley.

Hayley knew he had only unleashed a tiny fraction of his rage toward her.

There was a lot more to come.

Maybe it was a good thing that he hadn't come back into the room yet.

Especially since Maria seemed to enjoy what her husband was doing to her. If she liked it, she could have it, the longer Jay left her alone the more time it gave Brian, Adam, and Jessica to find her.

Finding a way to escape wasn't an option. Even if she wasn't restrained, Hayley wasn't sure she would have the strength to search the room for a weapon or try to break the window and climb out. They were on the second floor, and she wouldn't have been able to coordinate herself well enough to climb down, and she'd have to get Kinsley down as well. The only option would be to jump, which would only cause her more injuries, and it wasn't like she could throw a five-year-old out the window, nor could she leave her behind.

So, for now, they were stuck here, waiting, and to try to calm her nerves she may as well try to focus on something else.

"Kinsley, the night that Leah died, in your picture Leah was on the ground, your daddy was on the roof, you were in your bedroom, looking out the window. Where was your mommy?"

"She was outside," Kinsley replied.

"Before or after Leah went out the window and up onto the roof?"

"When Daddy went out the window after Leah, he told Mommy to go outside."

Interesting. Jay might not have necessarily planned on killing Leah when he followed her out onto the roof. If he'd told his wife to go outside, then he thought there was a chance that Leah might have gotten away and wanted to make sure Maria didn't let that happen.

So, Maria really was involved in the abuse of her children.

She had picked which side she was on, and it wasn't out of fear it was because she liked what Jay was doing to her. Hayley could tell when she looked into the woman's eyes. She could hear it in her voice and feel it in the air when the three of them had been in the back of the truck together. She had felt Maria Turner's jealousy. She'd seen the look on the woman's face when Jay had bent her over his knee and spanked her.

"Hayley?"

"Yes, honey?"

"Did my daddy hurt you?"

There was no point in lying to the child, even at five Kinsley knew what kind of man her father was. "Yes, he did."

"Is he going to hurt you again?"

"Probably."

"I want to leave," Kinsley said, her voice wobbling. So far, the little girl had done a marvelous job of holding it together, but she was just a child, and Hayley herself was finding it hard enough to stay strong, expecting Kinsley to was out of the question. Maybe she should tell the little girl to go out the window. It was a risky trek for such a small child, but realistically probably no riskier than her remaining here. The best they could hope for was that Jay and Maria had a lot of missed time to make up for and that they would spend another few hours together, which would buy enough time for Brian and the others to find them.

She couldn't let herself believe that she wouldn't be found.

She couldn't.

Because if she did, then she would lose all hope.

And if she lost all hope then she would fall apart.

She had to stay strong.

She had survived so much already, and she would survive this too. After all, she had the best motivation in the world to return home.

Brian.

The two of them had only just become a couple, she couldn't die now.

An ominous feeling filled the room, and a moment later the door opened, and Jay and Maria appeared.

Kinsley whimpered and pressed closer. The extra pressure on her battered body hurt, but Hayley didn't push the child away, instead, she drew her closer as though the little girl's sweet innocence could somehow protect her.

"It's time," Jay sneered. He carried in his hands a plank of wood and a couple of bricks. Maria also carried a few bricks. From the way the woman held herself Hayley knew she'd been right and that her husband had given her another brutal beating.

She didn't bother pointing out that he had Kinsley back now so there wasn't really any point in killing her because she knew it made no difference to him. Jay didn't care about his daughter beyond using her as a punching bag, and to him the point was that she had taken Kinsley to begin with.

Setting the plank of wood and the bricks beside the bed, Jay stood over her. His blue eyes were cold, icy cold, and she shivered as he fixed them on her in an unbreakable stare.

"Kinsley, go to your mother," Jay ordered.

The child hesitated, clinging tightly, her little cheeks wet with tears. But she obviously knew what disobedience would lead to and reluctantly stood and crossed the room to stand with Maria.

Jay leaned down and cut the rope securing her wrist to the bed, then roughly grabbed her by the arms and lifted her up, dropping her onto the mattress. Before she had a chance to try to move away, he had taken one of her arms and secured it to the bedpost. He repeated this with her other limbs. Pain radiated through her as her extended limbs put pressure on her injuries. She sucked in a breath and fought back the tears, she didn't want to add to Jay Turner's pleasure by crying.

"Think you're a tough girl, huh?" Jay pressed his thumb against the gash on her head, causing her to wince. "Leah used to think she was a tough girl too, but her mother and I taught her a lesson. I think this will work quite well for you." He picked up the plank of wood and set it on her chest. Then he picked up one of the bricks and held it over the wood. "It can take days to suffocate as I slowly increase the weight on your chest," he said with a smile.

Fear raced around her body.

It quickly progressed to terror.

She was already injured, she doubted that she could last for days with a brick crushing her chest.

She wasn't going to last until Brian found her.

One day with him wasn't enough. She wanted more. She had wanted to spend an entire lifetime with the man she loved, and yet she'd been given a measly twenty-four hours.

It wasn't fair.

With an evil grin, Jay placed the brick onto the board, and immediately her breathing was hampered.

Hayley wished she had listened to Brian and stayed at the safehouse where the two of them could have been curled up in each other's arms or making love right this second, instead, she was about to suffer a horribly slow death.

3:37 A.M.

Finally, things were working out just the way he wanted.

Jay was buzzed and not just from the eight cans of beer he'd downed in the last hour.

Although that definitely played a part in his good mood, he thought as he tossed his head back and swallowed the last of can number nine in one gulp. He threw the can onto the couch behind him and then gestured at Maria.

She didn't need to be told what to do, she was well trained and immediately stopped what she was doing, collected the empty can, and took it with her into the kitchen to throw into the recycling. Then she returned promptly with another nice cold can of beer from the fridge.

Pleased with how his day was going, he cracked open the new can and started drinking.

Everything was nice and quiet.

Peaceful.

Hayley Hood was quiet in her room, too busy trying to breathe with three bricks on her chest to worry about making a sound. Maria was sitting on the floor with Kinsley, building with a box of Legos he'd found in the spare bedroom's closet.

Everything was as it should be.

Soon Hayley would be dead—a slow, excruciating, terrifying death that befitted what she'd done—then he, his wife, and his kid could move on. He was already thinking about where they would go and what they would do. He had a friend from school who ran a garage in a small town about two hours from here. Maybe he could go there and get a job. He knew a little about mechanics, enough to get by. Maria could school Kinsley at home, they couldn't risk enrolling her in the local school as they'd be on the run, and that would alert the cops as to where they were.

He was going to be keeping his foot on Kinsley. There was no way he was allowing her to turn out like her disobedient, outspoken older sister. Maybe he and Maria would even try for another kid. Hopefully a boy this time. Boys grew into men, strong, tough men, he thought he'd like to have a son, someone to carry on the family name.

Content, Jay stretched back on the couch. This was the life. Lounging around, drinking beer while his wife attended to their child and his every need. The move was going to do them all good. Maybe they'd buy a farm, he liked the idea of a large property, of privacy and seclusion, where there would be no nosy neighbors who didn't understand butting in and sticking their noses where they didn't belong. No one would think to look for them in a small, quiet, sleepy town, and he would be free to do whatever he wanted with his family.

Yes, this was the life.

"Maria," he said.

She looked over but didn't speak, she knew better than to open her mouth without being given express permission to do so.

"I think the kid should go to bed now. Put her in the room across the hall from Hayley's. Once you've put her to sleep, wait for me in the master bedroom," Jay rattled off orders. He didn't need to elaborate on how he expected to find his wife waiting for him, she really was well trained.

It wasn't as easy as you might think to train a woman.

Even one as willing to learn as Maria was.

He'd never thought he'd meet a woman like her. It was like she had sensed the evil and violence that lurked inside him and that was exactly what had drawn her to him.

She wasn't like his mother or sister who had feared his father. She thrived from every slap he gave her, lived for every beating, and enjoyed every time he used her so roughly she was left bleeding and barely able to stand.

She was one of a kind.

He knew that she had grown up in a home with abuse, just like he had, although her stepfather had never laid a hand on her, but he didn't know how that had created the woman she had become.

Nor did he care.

All he cared about was that he had the perfect wife.

He'd go take a nice, hot shower, then tend to the two gunshot wounds he'd gotten in the last few days. Then he would check in on Hayley, maybe add another brick to the three already slowly crushing her chest, before going to the bedroom and letting Maria tend to his every whim.

Maria had picked up Kinsley and was just passing by him to walk down the hall to the staircase that led to the bedrooms when the front door was suddenly rammed open.

Without thinking about what he was doing, Jay just reacted. He grabbed Kinsley from her mother's arms and held her in front of him. Pinned to his chest, her small body was a barrier between himself and whoever had just broken in.

"Hands where we can see them," a voice yelled as three people rushed into the room. "Down on your knees, let the child go, hands in the air."

Jay ignored those orders.

No one told him what to do, especially not some woman cop.

He remembered two of the three people in the room. Detective Jessica Spears and Detective Adam Abram had been the cops there with Hayley Hood the day they had taken his kid. If he had his gun on him, he would have shot the two cops and the other man—who he thought was the one who had tried to stop him in the street last night after he'd crashed the stolen truck into Hayley's car. The man had nearly interrupted the abduction, probably would have if he hadn't been planning on setting the car on fire with the bodyguard still inside. If he had his gun, he definitely would have shot all three of them and not regretted it one iota.

"Jay Turner, put your daughter down and get onto the floor on your knees, hands above your head," the male cop ordered.

He just chuckled.

He wasn't going to do that.

He might not have his gun on him—having left it upstairs in the master bedroom—but he had an adorable little human shield that he knew none of the three people who had just broken in here would dare risk harming.

"I don't think so, Detective," he said with a smile.

"More officers will be arriving shortly. You're not walking away from here so you may as well surrender, save yourself additional charges," Detective Spears told him.

What a joke.

He had killed his daughter, he had attempted to kill Hayley Hood on multiple occasions, he had assaulted a bodyguard or cop or whoever the man was at the group home, he had tried to kill the bodyguard in the car last night, he had abducted his daughter, he had beaten his wife on several occasions, and he had Hayley Hood upstairs tied to a bed with bricks on her chest. There was no way he could cause himself more problems by refusing to surrender. By the time they added up all his charges he was probably never seeing the outside of a prison cell for the rest of his life, so he had nothing to lose.

"How did you find me?"

"A social worker got involved with your family after your father smashed your older sister's face into a mirror. Once your sister was removed from the home that left you as the next in line to take the brunt of your father's anger. You couldn't blame him for what he did, you're just like him, but you blamed your mother, your sister, and the social worker. Is Bridie Kocsh still alive?" Detective Spears asked.

He was getting annoyed.

He didn't like the attitude of the cops.

They thought they had gotten the best of him just because they had figured out where he was hiding.

So what?

That didn't make them better than him, and it didn't mean they were going to best him.

"Maria, down on your knees," Detective Spears ordered.

No way was that happening.

No one but him told his wife what to do.

"Maria, don't move," he commanded.

They were going to get his wife cuffed and out of here, and then it was just him and Kinsley. Then they would try to badger him into letting go of the only thing keeping him from being shot right now. They would try to distract him with talk about his past, trying to analyze it and find a way to explain why he had turned out to be the man he was.

But he didn't care about that.

He was who he was, he made no apologies for it.

And he wasn't going to let them use it as a weapon to keep his attention on them while they got their cop buddies to sneak into the house and take him out from behind.

Maria was too well trained to obey the command of anyone but him, and she still stood beside him, right where she'd been when the intruders had arrived.

A plan was already forming in his head.

A way where he got out of here and succeeded in ending Hayley Hood's life. If he played things right, he might also walk away with his wife and kid.

All he had to do was get upstairs to his gun. Then he'd run into Hayley's room, shoot her, then as the cops took Maria and Kinsley outside he could shoot them, then go out the window and flee.

He had to hurry though.

He had no doubt that the cops were telling the truth when they'd said that more of them were coming.

Without wasting another second, Jay threw Kinsley at Maria and ran.

3:58 A.M.

If they weren't right this time, he didn't think he could take it.

Brian was pretty much at the end of his rope.

One tiny little push and he was going to go tumbling over the edge and fall apart.

Hayley had been with that man for nearly twelve hours now. That was more than enough time for him to have killed her, and it was more than enough time for him to have tortured her.

That was almost more terrifying than the thought of Hayley being dead.

A quick death was one thing, he would never get over losing her, and neither would the rest of her family, but at least she wouldn't have suffered. But to think of her alone, scared, in pain, being tortured, that was too much. He couldn't cope with that. He couldn't. He needed her to be okay.

Brady, Adam, and Jessica had ordered him to stay in the car while they went inside to see if Jay Turner was hiding out with Hayley, his wife, and his daughter at the house of a woman named Bridie Kocsh. Bridie had been a social worker who had worked with Jay's family when he was a child. So far, he had complied, mainly because his body was physically fatigued. After not sleeping the night before, then the car accident, and worrying over Hayley, he was tapped out. And sore, his body ached, and the bumps, bruises, cuts, and broken nose were starting to make themselves known.

He just wanted Hayley back.

Now.

But they'd been wrong once already tonight.

They'd thought that Jay Turner might be staying at the home of a different retired social worker, but when they'd turned up the woman had been at home with her three sons and their families who were visiting from out of state. Since they thought that the anger he had directed toward Hayley had to come from a deeper seated place than just her doing her job and removing Kinsley from the home they decided to see if there was a social worker in his own past.

There was.

And now they were here.

Where he had been left waiting.

Shoving open the car door, Brian got out and began to pace up and down the sidewalk.

What was going on in there?

What was taking so long?

Was Jay Turner armed? Was that why Adam and Jessica hadn't arrested him already? There were three of them to Jay's one. They had the numbers, surely it wouldn't be much longer.

Was Hayley in there or had Jay left her someplace else?

Or dumped her dead body in a shallow grave, or at the side of a road, or in a dumpster somewhere?

There was a light on in an upstairs window.

Hayley.

For some reason, Brian knew she was in there.

He couldn't explain it, he just knew, he *felt* it, felt her. Just like he felt that she needed him. He had to go to her. Now. Waiting for Adam, Jessica, and Brady to finish doing whatever they were doing wasn't an option.

There was a trellis running up the side of the house underneath the window with the light on, he was pretty sure that he could make it up there relatively easily.

Spurred on by fear, he clambered up the wall as quickly as he could. It didn't take long, and when he reached the window, he shoved it open and climbed through. Then he froze.

He'd been right.

Hayley *was* inside the room.

She was tied, spread-eagled, to the bed. There was a plank of wood on her chest. On the plank of wood sat three bricks.

Hayley's face was ashen.

There were small dots of foam at the sides of her mouth.

Her eyes were closed.

Her breathing was labored, harsh gasps, wheezing in and out of her mouth as her lungs were compressed limiting the amount of air that could enter.

She was dying.

Slowly and painfully.

His ability to move returned and Brian ran to the bed, grabbing the bricks and dropping them onto the carpet. With the pressure off her chest, Hayley's breathing improved, but only slightly. Brian pressed his fingertips to her neck and felt her pulse fluttering weakly. At least she was still breathing. He'd gotten to her in time, but had he waited until the others had Jay Turner in handcuffs it might have been too late.

Pulling a small Swiss army knife from his pocket, Brian sawed quickly through the ropes binding Hayley to the bed. The second he had her free, he sat on the mattress and pulled her into his arms.

"Hayley?" he whispered, stroking her hair and rocking her gently from side to side. "Can you hear me?"

She didn't reply.

Just lay limply in his grasp.

"Come on, sweetheart," he begged. He needed her to wake up. He needed her to be okay. Losing her would crush him just as certainly as those bricks had been crushing Hayley's chest.

Tears brimmed in his eyes.

He loved this woman so completely. It might have taken him a while to realize what she meant to him, but now he knew. He loved her with the kind of love that could last an entire lifetime.

Losing Hayley wouldn't just be losing her but losing everything they could have had together. It would be losing a wife, children, grandchildren, years of happiness and laughter. It would be losing his life as well as hers.

A tear splashed down and dropped onto Hayley's pale cheek.

She stirred. Moved ever so slightly, a small, pained moan escaping her dry, chapped lips.

To Brian it was the most beautiful sound he had ever heard because it was a sign of life.

"Hayley." He brushed her hair back off her face, then took her face between his hands, his thumbs brushing lightly backward and forward across her cheekbones.

"Brian," she murmured, so softly he could hardly hear her. Then her eyelashes fluttered, and her eyes cracked open. "You came."

"You knew I would," he rebuked. "Nothing on this earth could keep me away from you. Nothing."

She gave a small smile, then her eyelids slid down, and she rested heavily against him.

"Just keep your breathing slow and steady," he told her. Hayley needed an ambulance, but they were stuck in here until Jay Turner was in custody. "Slow and steady," he repeated.

Hayley nodded, then just lay in his arms and rested.

He just held her, rocked her, stroked her hair, and tried to believe that she was okay, that she had survived, that they could still have the future they had talked about when they'd laid in each other's arms the other night.

Brian didn't know how long they sat there, but all of a sudden, the quiet night was pierced by the sound of a gun being fired.

It could have been Jessica, Adam, or Brady firing at Jay Turner, or it could have been Jay firing at them. Not willing to risk Hayley's safety, Brian stood with Hayley in his arms, knelt down, and pushed her under the bed.

"Don't come out. No matter what," he ordered.

Scared blue eyes looked back at him, but she nodded.

He went and hid behind the door. He'd barely gotten there when it swung open, and a man came storming in.

It wasn't one of his friends, it was Jay Turner, and he gasped when he saw the bed was empty. Obviously noticing the open window, he ran to it. Brian weighed up his options. He saw a gun in Jay's hands, and he was unarmed and injured. Jay had been shot twice over the last few days, but from the looks of things the wounds were superficial, he didn't move like he was in any pain.

The odds might be stacked against him, but if he did nothing, Jay was going to find Hayley.

There was some sort of commotion going on downstairs, so he wasn't sure how long it would be before someone came up to help.

His hand curled around the knife he'd used to cut Hayley free. If he could strike before Jay noticed him, he could kill the man. It was a quicker death than he deserved—a quicker death than the man had tried to give Hayley—but at least he'd be dead, and there would be some sort of justice in the world.

He crept from his hiding place, knife poised, but just as he stepped up behind the other man, Jay spun around.

"You," Jay spat out. "You took her from me."

Jay lifted his weapon but instead of firing it, he slammed it into Brian's temple. The force of the blow sent him sprawling onto the floor.

"You'll pay for messing with what's mine," Jay snarled, lifting the weapon once again, but this time aiming it directly at his head.

Brian wasn't afraid to die, the only thing he was afraid of was that Jay would find Hayley and kill her before the others could get up here.

He couldn't let that happen, but he didn't know how to stop it.

Then all of a sudden, a hand flew out from underneath the bed, wrapped around Jay's ankle, and yanked, sending the man falling.

Brian still held the knife, poised between them, and Jay landed on it as he fell, the blade slicing clean through his heart.

It took only a minute for the man to bleed out.

By then footsteps were pounding on the stairs.

Brian didn't care about them, and he didn't care that Jay was dying. He just shoved the man's body off him and scrambled to the bed, reaching under to pull Hayley out.

She'd just saved his life.

"Brian?" Adam sounded surprised as he came bursting through the door. "What are you doing here?"

He didn't have time to explain that right now, so Brian just said, "He's dead. Hayley needs an ambulance. Now."

Adam didn't ask any more questions, just yanked out his phone, and Brian brought Hayley with him as he shuffled backward on his bottom to rest against the wall. Cradling Hayley in his lap, they clung to each other, her still breathing heavily and erratically, but breathing.

They were both alive.

And that was all that mattered.

～

4:30 P.M.

• • •

"I don't think we should be here."

"We have to be," Hayley said. "If anyone ever deserved a merry Christmas it's Samara. She's our friend, and Michael asked us to come over and help surprise her, we have to be here."

"I think the fact that you spent the majority of the day in the hospital after nearly being suffocated to death exempts you," Brian said.

Hayley smiled at him. She knew he was worried about her. The last twenty-four hours had been as bad for him as they'd been for her. She couldn't imagine the fear he'd felt knowing she was with someone who wanted to kill her. She knew how she would have felt if their positions had been reversed. She would have felt like someone had wrapped a rope around her heart and was squeezing it until the life was crushed out of it.

But they were alive.

Both of them.

Back in the house when Brian had come rushing in to save her, she'd been sure that Jay was going to shoot him and then kill her too. She had been more afraid about Jay hurting Brian than herself, he'd already beaten and tried to kill her, but she couldn't let him do that to Brian, she couldn't let him take the man she loved away from her.

Finding reserves of strength she hadn't known she had left, she'd managed to unbalance Jay, sending him falling straight onto Brian's knife.

Not before Brian had been hurt though.

"Hey, you had to be treated at the hospital too," she reminded Brian.

"For a few bumps and bruises," he countered.

"And a concussion."

"You have a concussion too," he shot back. "And some cracked ribs, which mean you should be at home, in bed, resting."

"Well, you have a broken nose. Broken bones trump cracked bones." Brian opened his mouth to come back with another retort, then they both looked at each other and laughed. "Are we really arguing over who is hurt worse?"

"I think we are." Brian wrapped an arm around her shoulders and pulled her close. "I'm just worried about you. I nearly lost you."

Hayley felt the shudder that rippled through his body.

She could feel the fear that hadn't quite dissipated yet. She wished she could wipe away the last day and make it so it never happened, but she couldn't, and neither of them would ever forget this day.

Every time she closed her eyes or her mind wandered, she found herself back in that bedroom, tied to the bed, the bricks on her chest slowly crushing her to death. Her breath would start to hitch, just as it had back in the bedroom. She could hear it wheezing in and out of her lungs as she struggled to get in enough oxygen, fighting for every breath she took.

She could feel her pulse pounding.

Feel that same terror that had filled her.

Hayley didn't think that horror would ever leave her.

"Hey." Brian trailed his fingers up and down her arm. "You're hyperventilating. Try to calm down. Breathe slowly with me."

Letting Brian's calm voice guide her, she latched onto it and slowly her breathing began to ease.

"You okay?" he asked when she could breathe normally again.

"I was just thinking about today, in Jay's house," she said softly.

"Try not to think about it." Brian kissed the top of her head.

"I can't stop."

"I know, me either, but today is Christmas Eve. Jay Turner is dead, Maria Turner is in prison, Kinsley is back at the group home, and we're both alive. Everything worked out okay. It's just going to take time for us to process it all, for us to work our way through it. But we'll be okay, know why?"

"Why?"

"Because we have each other. Every time I picture you tied to that bed, I just look at you, and I see that you're okay, and eventually that'll sink in. Every time you get scared and can't stop thinking about it, you just look at me, and you know what, I'll be here. I'm not going anywhere, not now, not ever. I got a little taste of what my life would be like without you, and I hated it. From here on out, it's you and me, together, always. I don't want to live without you. Any time you're struggling you just remember that."

Hayley smiled at him and snuggled closer, tucking her head onto Brian's shoulder. "Okay. Thank you."

"Don't ever thank me for loving you. I should be thanking you for not giving up on me. It took me a while to get to the same place you were in, and if you'd given up and moved on then we wouldn't be together right now."

"I could never have given up on you," she said, taking Brian's hands and entwining their fingers. "I love you."

"And I love you. Which is why I think we should ask Brady to drive us home. We can sit in bed, watch Christmas movies, drink hot chocolate, eat some of Savannah Crane's Christmas cookies, and you can get the sleep you need."

As lovely as that sounded, there would be time to do it later. Right now, this was where she wanted to be. She and Brian might have had a bad twenty-four hours, but Samara Patrick had had a horrendous year, and she needed this. "This is Samara's chance to have what we have, our families and all our friends are here, this is something I want to do. Something I *need* to do." Hayley needed something to do to take her out of her head for a while, and this was the perfect thing.

"All right," Brian conceded. "I guess we can find something non-strenuous to do."

"Thanks for understanding."

Hand in hand, they climbed out of the back of Brady's car and headed into Samara Patrick's house. The place and the yard were buzzing as fifty-odd people worked to turn the house into a winter wonderland before Samara came home with Michael. Hayley hoped it was enough to help the couple reunite. Despite the rocky road they'd had, Hayley knew they were great together and could find a way to move forward and be happy.

"Two more worker bees," Brian said to Samara's brother Fin as they stepped inside. "Where do you need us?"

"Since you two look like you could fall over any second, why don't you go unpack the boxes with the Christmas tree decorations and lay them out on the table," Fin told them.

Heading into the living room, she and Brian sat side by side on the couch and began to unwrap decorations. There were four big boxes of them. Hayley wasn't sure where they all came from, she knew that Samara didn't celebrate Christmas—or at least she hadn't before—but maybe after seeing this magical wonderland her house was turning into she would change her mind.

"Oh, look at this adorable little Santa and Mrs. Claus," she said as she opened the first box and picked up one of the decorations sitting on top, unwrapping the tissue paper it was wrapped in. "They're kissing. How cute is that?"

"It's pretty cute," Brian agreed.

"And a reindeer, look it lights up," she said as she opened the next one and pressed the little button on its stomach that made its little nose glow red.

"Also cute."

"Aww, this angel has little feathers for wings." Hayley unwrapped the next decoration.

"Are you going to get excited about every single decoration you unwrap?" Brian asked, amused.

"Probably." Hayley grinned. "This is the third tree I've decorated this year. The one in my house, then the one in the safehouse, and now this one."

"Maybe next year we'll be decorating a tree of our own. Together," Brian said.

Those nervous butterflies she was getting used to started fluttering in her stomach. "You mean a tree that's both of ours?"

"Yes."

"Because it's in a house that we live in together?"

"Yes."

"Are you asking me to move in with you?" Brian had talked about it in the car on the way to Jay's house, but they'd been interrupted before he could outright ask her.

A corner of Brian's mouth quirked up in a half smile. "I obviously need to work on making myself clearer, but yes, that's what I'm asking."

This was a dream come true for her. She wanted to say yes, but was this too soon? Was it the right thing to do? Should she be making big life-altering decisions on the back of such a traumatic experience?

Although she had trained herself out of it over the last twenty years, letting her head and not her emotions guide her, Hayley knew this was one time she had to let her heart make the decision.

"Yes."

"Yes?" Brian arched a brow.

"Yes." She threw her arms around his neck and kissed him without any regard for the fact that her whole family—her parents and little sister as well as Brian's parents—were all here and watching.

A cheer went up around the room, and she broke the kiss, laughing even as her cheeks turned bright red.

"Okay, okay, show over," Brian said.

"I really love you," she told Brian as everyone went back to what they'd been doing.

"I really love you too, and if we didn't have concussions and a patchwork of bruises over our bodies, I'd show you how much when we get home."

"I think we can find something we can do," she said, giving Brian another quick kiss. "But now we have to get these decorations ready to put on the tree."

"You are such a tease," Brian muttered, fighting a grin as he returned to unpacking the decorations.

Hayley laughed. This was just the kind of day she loved the most, her family together, Christmas just hours away, and the man she loved sitting beside her. She might be tired, sore, and still a little breathless, but this was definitely turning out to be one of the best Christmases she'd ever had.

# CHAPTER
## *Seven*

December 25th
2:22 A.M.

It was good to be home.

Although it had only been a little over twenty-four hours since he and Hayley had last been alone together, it felt like an eternity.

So much had changed in that time.

And yet, at the same time, it felt like everything was just the same.

When they'd left the safehouse, he knew that he was in love with Hayley, and he knew that he wanted to spend the rest of his life with her, but going through what they had, fearing for her safety, experiencing what it would be like to lose her, his love for her had grown so much in these thirty-six hours.

"Thanks, Brady," he said as his friend pulled to a stop outside his house.

"Anytime. You two going to be okay tonight?" Brady asked. "You both do have concussions so if you need me to stay. Or you want to take Paige and Elias or Daisy and Mark up on their offers to have you two spend the night? I'm happy to drive you to either of their houses."

No way.

He wanted Hayley all to himself tonight.

"We'll be fine, but thank you," Brian answered. "You want to stay here tonight, right?" he asked Hayley because as much as he wanted it to be just the two of them if she wanted to spend the night at her parents' house they would.

"Oh, yeah." She winked at him, and he immediately thought of her declaration at Samara's house that despite their concussions and injuries they could find something to do to make out a little when they got home.

Brady laughed, apparently knowing exactly what they were talking about. "Okay, you two have fun, but be careful, and call someone if you need anything."

They would, although he was a doctor and perfectly capable of monitoring himself and Hayley overnight. "Goodnight, Brady, and thank you for everything you've done the last few days."

"Anytime. Merry Christmas."

"Merry Christmas," he and Hayley said as they climbed out of the car.

Walking down the path to the front door felt different, they hadn't discussed yet whether Hayley was going to move in with him, or he was going to move in with Hayley, or they were going to look for a new place together, but wherever they ended up living this would always be where they spent their first Christmas together.

Brian unlocked the front door and switched on the lights as they stepped inside. They both looked around, a little lost now that they were finally home after everything they'd gone through. He wanted to feel safe, Jay Turner was dead, the threat hanging over Hayley's head was gone, and yet the tension he'd been living with this last week was still there. He knew it was for Hayley too. Every time his mind wasn't occupied with something else it drifted back to find Hayley in that bedroom. He knew she kept thinking about it too. She'd started hyperventilating back at Samara's house, and he was sure it was because she was having flashbacks.

He wanted to take away all the suffering she had endured, it killed him that he couldn't. He didn't want her to ever be scared, hurt, or feel pain of any kind. He would a hundred times over take that pain himself so that she didn't have to endure it if he could.

Before he could let their good moods drop, he spotted a sprig of mistletoe hanging above them.

That was perfect.

He wrapped an arm around Hayley's waist and drew her up against him, touching his lips to hers and kissing her very lightly. She responded immediately, and before he knew it the kiss had turned hot and passionate, and he was closing the door behind them and pushing her up against it. His hands spanned her waist, her fingers curled in his hair, and the kiss grew deeper, more than just a kiss. Emotion and love passed between them.

Despite the fact that he knew it wasn't a good idea, medically speaking, to take things any further than a kiss, Brian knew that this kiss was quickly going to turn into something a whole lot more.

Hayley's hands dropped to his waist, unzipping his jeans and shoving them down his hips. He returned the favor by pushing her sweatpants, along with her panties, down, then carefully lifted her up, easing her down onto him, never breaking the kiss.

Just being inside Hayley was enough to push him right to the edge, but he needed them to come at the same time. As he thrust upward, he held her weight with one arm, then reached between them, touching her as he continued to thrust upward. It didn't take either of them long to reach that place, and less than a minute later he thrust one last time and Hayley gasped, then a split second later, his world exploded into a million brightly colored stars.

"That was a mistake," he said, breathing heavily as he slowly floated back to earth.

"Didn't feel like it." Hayley giggled.

"It will in the morning when we're both too sore to move, and we have to go to the family Christmas gathering," he countered.

"We didn't use a condom again," Hayley said, sobering.

"No, we didn't." It probably wasn't very responsible of them, but the idea of a little person, half him and half Hayley, running around was too appealing for him to care.

Yanking up his pants, he pushed Hayley's back up, then scooped her into his arms and carried her to the sofa, grabbing a blanket and covering them both as he sat with her on his lap. Something had happened to change Hayley's mood, and he knew it wasn't the fantastic sex they'd just had.

"What's wrong?" he asked, rubbing small circles on her back with his hand.

"I'm not sure I should have said yes when you asked me to move in with you," she said in a small voice.

Panic sliced through him. "What? Why?"

"Because ..." she paused, shifting slightly, trying to pull away from him.

He wasn't going to let her do that.

Whatever was bothering her they were going to deal with together because they were a couple now. Whatever affected her affected him.

Tightening his hold on her, he asked, "Because what, sweetheart?"

"There's no other family to take Kinsley. I don't want her to go to a foster home. If it wasn't for my parents, I don't know what would have happened to me if I'd entered the system, and I don't want that life for Kinsley. She's already been through so much. I want her to have a family, parents who love her, and more siblings one day. Brian, I want to look into fostering her and then adopting her. I want to give her what my parents gave me and Arianna. But I can't ask you to do that."

He relaxed, resuming rubbing circles on her back. "Why couldn't you ask me to do that?"

"Because we're talking about raising a child. A *traumatized* child. That's a lot to take on."

"You're sure?"

"About raising Kinsley? Yes."

"Then I'm in too. We're a couple now, nothing is going to make me leave you, certainly not that great, big heart of yours."

"Really?" She looked up at him with those gorgeous big blue eyes, and he knew there wasn't anything he wouldn't do just to make her smile.

"Really."

"Just like that? You'd take on raising Kinsley with me?"

"Of course. She's a sweet little girl, and we can give her the home she needs to grow up to be just like you."

"I didn't think it was possible, but I think I love you more." Hayley tilted her face up and kissed him.

"I have something for you. A Christmas gift, but I don't want to wait until later today to give it to you." Sliding Hayley off his lap, he switched on the Christmas tree lights, then reached underneath to pull out a small candy cane striped box.

"Thank you." Hayley beamed as she took the box.

She undid the bright red, curly ribbon, then removed the lid. Inside was a smaller box; it was blue, the same shade as Hayley's eyes. She lifted the lid off the second box, and her eyes grew watery as she began to take out the things resting inside.

"These are all from my past," she looked up at him, unshed tears shimmering in the light of the Christmas tree.

"I spoke with your mom a couple of months ago and asked her to help me find as many old clothes and things from your childhood as we could. Then I cut them all up into squares. There's the dress you were wearing the day we all met you, dresses from special occasions in your past, first Christmas, first birthday you spent with your parents, high school graduation, college graduation. There are squares from the sleeping bag you used to use when we went camping, the blanket you used to sit under when you had family movie nights, picnic blankets, and your old dog Bubble's blanket. I thought that since you love to sew you could make them into a quilt for your bed, like a memory quilt, something that you could keep adding to over the years with other special things. I didn't know that things would turn out like this, but since your old quilt got burned when Jay Turner attacked your house now you can make a new one."

"Brian," she sobbed out his name as she threw herself into his arms. "This is the most thoughtful gift I've ever been given. I love it. I want to start sewing it right now. I just wish that the clothes I'd been wearing the other night when you told me you loved me for the first time hadn't been ruined with blood from the car accident, and Jay beating me. I would have loved to have them as part of my new special quilt."

"I knew you would want that." Gently he eased her off his chest and sat her back up, then he went to the table and grabbed an envelope. "I asked Adam and Jessica to get me a piece of your sweater. The rest is in evidence, but Jay is dead, and they have your statement and a whole bunch of other evidence, so they were able to get me a piece of it. A non-bloody piece." He gave it to her, and fresh tears trickled down her cheeks.

"I love you so much. All these years I prayed that you would love me back, and now that you do it's so much better than I could ever have imagined."

Brian sat beside her and pulled her back into his lap. "I love you too. And even though I wish I'd known sooner that I was going to fall in love with you, I think our relationship is going to be even stronger because we've been such great friends for so long. I hope a baby is growing in here." He placed his hand on her stomach. "Then you, me, and Kinsley will have another member of our family to love."

"Family." She sighed contentedly and snuggled closer. "I love the sound of that word. My parents gave me the perfect family to grow up in, and now you and I are going to have a family of our own. Even if I'm not pregnant, I will be one day, and we'll have our very own little baby to love. And Kinsley, we are going to smother her with love, so she never feels unsafe or unloved ever again. Christmas was the first real holiday I celebrated with my new family when I was adopted, and it's always been my favorite holiday, but now I love it so much more. Merry Christmas, Brian."

"Merry Christmas, my sweet, beautiful Hayley, I love you so much, and I feel so lucky that I get to love you every day for the rest of my life."

Christmas had always been his favorite holiday, ever since he could remember, but Hayley was right, sitting here together, in the early hours of Christmas morning, the Christmas tree lights twinkling brightly, knowing that they were at the beginning of their journey as a couple, that they would soon have a family of their own, and that the magic of the season had played a part in them getting here, now he loved it even more.

. . .

**Check out my River's End Rescues series for small town romantic suspense, with action and mystery, family and friendship, and of course, serial killers!**

Some Regrets Are Forever (River's End Rescues #1)

# Also by Jane Blythe

Detective Parker Bell Series

A SECRET TO THE GRAVE

WINTER WONDERLAND

DEAD OR ALIVE

LITTLE GIRL LOST

FORGOTTEN

Count to Ten Series

ONE

TWO

THREE

FOUR

FIVE

SIX

BURNING SECRETS

SEVEN

EIGHT

NINE

TEN

Broken Gems Series

CRACKED SAPPHIRE

CRUSHED RUBY

FRACTURED DIAMOND

SHATTERED AMETHYST

SPLINTERED EMERALD

SALVAGING MARIGOLD

River's End Rescues Series

COCKY SAVIOR

SOME REGRETS ARE FOREVER

SOME FEARS CAN CONTROL YOU

SOME LIES WILL HAUNT YOU

SOME QUESTIONS HAVE NO ANSWERS

SOME TRUTH CAN BE DISTORTED

SOME TRUST CAN BE REBUILT

SOME MISTAKES ARE UNFORGIVABLE

Candella Sisters' Heroes Series

LITTLE DOLLS

LITTLE HEARTS

LITTLE BALLERINA

Storybook Murders Series

NURSERY RHYME KILLER

FAIRYTALE KILLER

FABLE KILLER

Saving SEALs Series

SAVING RYDER

SAVING ERIC

SAVING OWEN

SAVING LOGAN

SAVING GRAYSON

SAVING CHARLIE

Prey Security Series

PROTECTING EAGLE

PROTECTING RAVEN

PROTECTING FALCON

PROTECTING SPARROW

PROTECTING HAWK

PROTECTING DOVE

Prey Security: Alpha Team Series

DEADLY RISK

LETHAL RISK

EXTREME RISK

FATAL RISK

COVERT RISK

SAVAGE RISK

Prey Security: Artemis Team Series

IVORY'S FIGHT

PEARL'S FIGHT

LACEY'S FIGHT

OPAL'S FIGHT


Prey Security: Bravo Team Series


VICIOUS SCARS

RUTHLESS SCARS


Christmas Romantic Suspense Series


CHRISTMAS HOSTAGE

CHRISTMAS CAPTIVE

CHRISTMAS VICTIM

YULETIDE PROTECTOR

YULETIDE GUARD

YULETIDE HERO

HOLIDAY GRIEF


Conquering Fear Series (Co-written with Amanda Siegrist)


DROWNING IN YOU

OUT OF THE DARKNESS

CLOSING IN

# About the Author

USA Today bestselling author Jane Blythe writes action-packed romantic suspense and military romance featuring protective heroes and heroines who are survivors. One of Jane's most popular series includes Prey Security, part of Susan Stoker's OPERATION ALPHA world! Writing in that world alongside authors such as Janie Crouch and Riley Edwards has been a blast, and she looks forward to bringing more books to this genre, both within and outside of Stoker's world. When Jane isn't binge-reading she's counting down to Christmas and adding to her 200+ teddy bear collection!

To connect and keep up to date please visit any of the following